The Cowboys of Cavern County

ISLA'S IRISH COWBOY

BELLA SETTARRA

Dedication

To Amy, with love xx
I would like to thank my lovely friends, Julieanne and
Leigh, from Belfast, Northern Ireland, for all their help
with the 'Irishisms' which I hope made Kean Maguire a
more believable character. Also, all my Irish online readers
who kindly gave me their opinions and advice about the
dialect. Unfortunately, I was not able to include much of
it in the story as the wider audience would be unfamiliar
with the terms and might think my book was full of typos
and grammatical errors, lol! My sincerest thanks, anyway.
Go raibh maith agat.

Books by Bella Settarra

The Cowboys of Cavern County

Carla's Cowboys
Maggie's Man
Two for Trinity
Isla's Irish Cowboy

Isla's Irish Cowboy

ISBN # 978-1-78686-315-7

©Copyright Bella Settarra 2017

Cover Art by Posh Gosh ©Copyright 2017

Interior text design by Claire Siemaszkiewicz

Totally Bound Publishing

Chapter One

"I still can't believe you're going through with this."

Isla Gillingham rolled her eyes for the umpteenth time as the large trailer sped past a road sign for Cavern County.

She sighed, tired of the same old argument.

"It'll ruin your image. Your career will be over, you know." Tabitha wasn't giving up — unfortunately.

"I think it will show how versatile I am. I've done all that high-end, city stuff and now I'm showing another side of me." Isla had given up worrying about what her manager, Tabitha Merchant, thought of her decision. For once in her life, she'd taken control and wasn't going to back down.

"All I can say is this Mary-Lou Trotter must be a very good friend of yours to make you go to all this trouble." Tabitha bit the words out of thin, tight lips, clearly holding back what she really wanted to say. Isla wondered, not for the first time, whether there wasn't more to this than the older lady was letting on.

"Actually, I've never met her," she replied, airily. "But Beryl Boothroyd is a lovely lady and she helped me when I needed it, so I'm happy to return the favor. It's what people do."

"It's what *country* people do, maybe." Tabitha sneered from the soft leather chair opposite her. She had made no secret of her distaste for the country, and it was really grating on Isla's last nerve now.

"Is there something wrong with that?" Isla gaped at her manager. She'd had about enough already. Her heart pounded as she geared herself for another row. She knew it would end in tears — hers, as usual — but she was fed up taking all this shit because she had agreed to take on a job that Tabitha Merchant didn't think worthy of her reputation.

"Look... All I'm saying is that you're *somebody* now, thanks to me. You've had your photos on the covers of *Vogue* and *Cosmo* more than once and you're making good money. I don't see why you should cut off your hair — which is actually one of your defining features — and waste nearly a week coming all this way to do a shoot for nothing. What the hell is that all about?" Tabitha raised her hands as well as her voice.

"It's all about helping each other!" Isla shouted at the older woman, who looked shocked, to say the least. "Beryl helped me when I was a struggling model, and now I've got the opportunity to help *her*. What don't you understand?"

Tabitha narrowed her mean, pale eyes, her whole face shriveling into a crone-like snarl. "Just because this woman gave you a leg-up before you became famous, doesn't mean she has a hold on you now. You've got your image to think of — an image that *I* helped create."

Isla huffed incredulously. "I'm not exactly what you'd call famous, and there is no way I want to portray the image of a spoiled brat. I'm a country girl, Tabitha — always have been, always will be. I might live and work in the city now, but that's only because that's where most of the work is. I'd move back to this sort of place in a heartbeat if I could."

"It would be the end of your career if you did."

Isla stared at her as the trailer pulled to a halt. "Well, perhaps that wouldn't be such a bad thing," she muttered through clenched teeth.

"This is it," Chad, the driver, called over to them.

Isla dragged her glare from the woman in front of her and looked out of the window. A feeling of calmness washed over her as she gazed at the mountains rising before them and she quickly slid from her seat and went outside to take a closer look.

"Well, this is different." Katie, the makeup artist sidled up to her, smiling. She'd arrived in one of the other trailers that had gotten there first, allowing the crew to set up before Isla arrived. Isla now wished she'd also come in an earlier trailer instead of enduring Tabitha's wrath for the past few hours.

"Isn't it?" Isla nodded.

The air was fresh and washed over her tight skin, while the smell of grass and trees filled her senses. The mountain looked cool and calm, somehow, and she was surrounded with an air of tranquility. She had missed this so much.

"We can get a couple of beautiful evening shots with the mountains in the background and the sun just beginning to set behind them," Stefan, the photographer, suggested eagerly.

Isla nodded. It was good to see that he was completely on board with the project. "Shall I change?"

"Only if you want to. I think the jeans and T-shirt look will be fine, though." Stefan grinned.

"Let's just run a comb through your hair." Alex, who was brilliant with hair and costuming, came toward her with her vanity case.

"Hmm, that won't take long," Tabitha sneered from behind them.

"Well, that can only be a good thing," Isla told her pointedly. "We don't want to lose the light and waste a whole day now, do we?"

Alex rolled her eyes and Isla was pleased to see she wasn't the only one getting mighty pissed at Tabitha's attitude toward her new look.

"We'll go inside." Isla ushered the stylist back to her trailer, glad to put some distance between them and her irritating manager.

"I don't know why you put up with her," Alex confided once they were alone.

Isla looked up at her through the mirror. "Neither do I." She thought for a moment. "I suppose I was just so grateful to her in the early days when she took me on that I feel some sort of obligation to her now."

"Ha! You'd have made it without her," Alex replied, teasing a little of her hair out of the curly cluster it had formed at the back of her head. "It was your looks and personality that got you where you are now, not her contacts. That woman's making a fortune off you and she knows it."

Isla sighed.

"She's still moaning about your hair, I see?" Alex chirped on. "*I* love it."

Isla smiled, studying her reflection. Her hair was now chin-length and the natural curls were more pronounced than when she'd worn it long. "Me too."

Katie arrived to touch up her makeup and, after swapping her Converse for cowboy boots, Isla was ready to go.

Stefan had already gotten the lights in place, and a generator roared in the background, surely scaring off the local wildlife. He smiled when he saw her. "Wow! You look beautiful, darlin'."

Isla grinned. Stefan always showered her in compliments, and it really used to buoy her confidence. He was a good-looking dude—the typical tall, dark and handsome guy every girl dreamed of—which made his flattery even more potent. Now she could see that it was all part of his job, but it was still good to hear. She toyed with a curl that tickled her ear and Stefan nodded.

"Love it."

She felt a little smug as she looked over to see Tabitha scowling. Everyone had raved about her new haircut except Tabitha. It had been Beryl's suggestion, as her friend, Mary-Lou Trotter, had wanted a particular look for her magazine shoot. Those particulars were written in the folder Stefan was checking now.

"Ready?"

Isla smiled. She was more than ready. She'd been looking forward to this shoot for weeks. It was a pity the same couldn't be said for Tabitha, but then, she had been told she didn't have to come. They could manage quite well without her. Tabitha was clearly not going to be left out of the loop, though. She was still seething that her own sister, Suzanne, had agreed to the shoot in her absence. Isla had, of course, planned it that way. She'd asked Suzanne while Tabitha had been away dealing with another client, and as the other partner in the firm, Suzanne had been happy to sign the agreement.

Isla took her position between two large lights that had been planted in the soft earth. She inhaled the fresh scent and closed her eyes momentarily as memories of a happy childhood ran through her mind.

"Lovely," she heard Stefan cooing.

She opened her eyes, surprised to see that he had already started snapping pictures.

A big smile spread over her face as she posed for the photos. Part-way through, Alex passed her a cowboy hat and a little later a tan leather jacket with soft tassels hanging from it.

Tabitha and some of the other crew had gone back to their trailers to keep warm when the cold wind began to bite with nightfall, but Isla was quite happy posing for as long as Stefan wanted.

She was lost in the smells of the open countryside, the views of the mountains and trees and the feeling of belonging.

It had been quite a few years since she'd left the country to pursue her career. Her looks had been spotted by a talent scout while she had still been at school and she'd been happy to go along with the little company and gain some experience — though not much pay — in the industry. Beryl Boothroyd had been at one of the networking dinners that the company ran, and her boss had been livid when Isla told him that the older lady, founder of a larger fashion house, had offered her a job that she intended to take.

Beryl had taken Isla under her wing and taught her loads about the fashion and modeling industries — things Isla knew would have taken her years to learn otherwise.

Unfortunately, Beryl had taken ill and had to retire early from her job. Isla's management was taken over by some of her team, but as the company began to flounder without Beryl's input, more and more of the staff had left and Isla had found her job not half as much fun or as lucrative as it once had been. Then the in-house magazine had begun to fold and, without sponsorship, the whole business had been set to close with it.

When Tabitha Merchant offered her the moon on a stick, Isla had jumped at the chance for a new start and moved over to her management, instead. At first, she had been happy to fall in with whatever Tabitha had wanted, believing that with her new manager's contacts and experience, the woman would be doing what was best for her. She had secured some work with some of the high-end magazines and Isla had even appeared on TV a couple of times in perfume advertisements. Tabitha seemed to be making more and more demands on her, however, and she was losing her love of the business. She often wondered whether moving to Tabitha's company hadn't simply meant jumping from the frying pan and into the fire.

When Beryl had contacted her a few months before to ask how she would feel about helping out a friend of hers over in Cavern County, Isla had readily agreed. Mary-Lou Trotter ran a local magazine that concentrated on fashion for the rural communities. It was quite an innovative idea and one that readers seemed to have embraced with an undying thirst. Mary-Lou was struggling to keep up with demand for new and unusual features, so when Beryl told her she had connections with Isla Gillingham, Mary-Lou had leaped at the chance to work with her.

Beryl had been completely upfront about the size of Mary-Lou's company and the limited funds it ran on, and Isla had been quite happy to offer her services free of charge. Tabitha, on the other hand, had hit the roof.

"Smile." Stefan's voice pulled her from her thoughts and

she realized she had been practically frowning.

"Sorry." She gave him a dazzling beam, suddenly remembering where she was, and once again breathed in the atmosphere.

Stefan chuckled. "The far-away look was pleasing to start with, darlin', but it got a bit fierce, I'm afraid," he told her. "No prizes for guessing who you were thinking about there."

Isla laughed. The whole crew saw the way Tabitha ordered her about and they had all remarked on it at one time or another.

A marquee had been erected on the grass a short distance from where they were working, and the smells of burgers and sausages wafted over, taunting them.

"I don't know about you, but I think it's supper time," Stefan announced after a while.

Isla let out a grateful 'yee-haw', playfully throwing the hat into the air in relief.

"Perfect." Stefan had continued to snap more photos while she did so, and she rolled her eyes. He was a brilliant photographer and never seemed to stop working. Some of her best shots had been taken by him when she hadn't been posing or expecting it. She supposed that was what made him so good.

Isla gazed up at the mountains that looked black against an inky-blue sky. In the distance, stars were appearing and she hugged herself happily. Living in the city, she hadn't actually seen the stars for a while, and she was surprised how much she'd missed them. There was a lot about the country that she missed, she realized.

She followed Stefan into the marquee, which was set up with tables, chairs and the cooking area at one end. A hot buffet had been laid out and Isla licked her lips at the spread available to them. She dutifully piled her plate high with fresh salad but couldn't resist adding a sausage and a few fries. Tabitha's eyes bore into the back of her head and she knew her manager wouldn't be happy if she put on a couple of pounds. Still, she'd been told they would be riding up into the mountains for some action shots over the next few days, so she was hoping to shed any excess weight that way. Eating while on location was always a challenge.

Stefan showed her a few of the photographs he'd taken while they ate. Isla was amazed how relaxed she looked. The setting sun had bounced off her blonde curls, adding a sort of halo in some of the shots. That, with the dreamy expression while she had been enjoying the scenery, made for some lovely pictures.

"The shorter hair frames your face beautifully," Stefan told her. "It really suits you, darlin'."

He must have noticed that Tabitha had just come to join them, and Isla smirked at the look of annoyance they received from the older lady.

"I've got your schedule for tomorrow," Tabitha announced, placing a folder on the table next to Isla's plate. "We've got an early start, so you should think about getting to bed as soon as you're ready. I've got a meeting with Ms. Trotter, who wants to go through her requirements and show me some of the locations she has in mind for the shoots. I just hope the weather holds."

Isla nodded, wiping her hands in a napkin before taking up the file. It was winter. There was a good chance they might be hindered with poor weather, but snow hadn't been forecast yet for this week, which was good. Isla had lots of warm clothes with her, and the trailers were surprisingly snug.

"At least you're not doing bikini shots," Stefan offered with a grin.

Isla rolled her eyes. "It's supposed to be fashionable wear for cowgirls," she reminded him, shaking her head. "I don't think we'll see many of them scantily clad around here, do you?"

"Not if they've got any sense," he agreed, giving her a cheeky wink.

"The people from one of the local ranches are coming to

speak to me about arrangements but they haven't organized a time." Tabitha looked disparagingly at the document that Isla was flicking through. "I hope it's not a sign of how things are done around here—slap-dash and shoddy."

"Which one's he then?" Isla asked, noticing a gorgeous hunk in a cowboy hat entering the marquee. Her stomach, which had roiled with anger a few seconds ago, was now burning with a totally different sensation.

Chapter Two

Kean Maguire took a deep breath before entering the large white marquee that had been erected on the southwest field. Not only was it ugly and incongruous, ruining the view of the beautiful countryside he had come to love here in Cavern County, but the massive trailers parked outside it had churned up the mud of what should have been good pasture for the animals. He sighed. Ben Fielding must know what he was doing, he guessed, and who was he to argue?

People were seated around at the tables, eating and chatting, and his stomach gurgled as he smelled the sausages and burgers cooking over an elaborate-looking barbeque at the far end of the marquee. *How the other half lives, eh?*

"Can we help you, son?" A smart-looking guy in his fifties with a bald head and narrow eyes walked up to him, almost barring his way.

Kean blinked at him slowly, conveying his disdain for the whole debacle.

"I'm from the Fielding Ranch. I've come to speak to someone in charge."

The guy looked a little taken aback, probably because of his curt manner, although Kean's broad Irish accent may have also been a factor. The man blustered a little, pouting. "What's it about?"

Kean sighed. This guy was clearly the gatekeeper around here. "Mr. Fielding has asked me to speak to whoever is running the show to discuss arrangements for tomorrow. Of course, it that's a problem, I can always—" He turned to go.

"No, no." The guy was clearly thrown by his attitude and quickly put out his hands in a placating manner. "You'll want to speak to Tabitha Merchant. She's Miss Gillingham's manager." He gestured toward a woman who appeared to be holding court at one of the tables.

Kean looked over at the officious-looking lady with the stern gray bob and perpetual sneer. She was talking with a couple of older guys, but it was the blonde beauty to her left who caught his eye. To call her beautiful would be a gross understatement. Her golden hair shone in the artificial light, framing her gorgeous face, her full mouth was slightly parted and her big brown eyes oozed warmth and vulnerability. What was more, those eyes were staring right back at him.

He tensed his jaw, reluctantly tearing his gaze from her to address the woman he had come to see.

"Tabitha, this guy's from the ranch. He's come to discuss arrangements for tomorrow," the man next to him offered, leading him toward the table.

Trying to ignore the burn in his stomach as he neared them, Kean forced himself to focus on the older woman. He removed his hat and nodded politely at her before quickly glancing around at the rest of her party. "Kean Maguire, madam. Mr. Fielding asked me to come and welcome you to the ranch. He's sorry he couldn't be here himself, but somethin' urgent has cropped up. He said he'll see you first thing in the mornin'."

Tabitha looked as though she had just smelled sour milk and Kean felt the telltale tic in his neck spring into action, indicating his annoyance. He took a deep breath and gritted his teeth as he held out a hand to shake hers.

"So, you're the errand boy, are you? I really thought your boss might have made himself available, but still, I'm sure you can pass on a few messages."

She'd ignored his hand completely. Kean let his breath out long and slowly, using the time to dampen the thoughts that were racing though his head. Her reaction wasn't a complete surprise. He'd known he was being sent on a fool's errand. This woman wouldn't want to deal with him. Why would she? After all, she was right on the money about him. He wasn't much more than an errand boy. But at least he was earning honest money for once. He was determined to hold on to this job at all costs and was darned if a stuck-up, city-dwelling bitch was going to lose it for him.

"Yes, madam. I can pass on whatever messages you'd like me to."

He heard a snigger from the two guys who sat at the opposite side of the table and the blonde beauty giggled. He glanced up at her to see that she had turned a bright shade of scarlet and was clearly trying to stop herself from laughing.

Tabitha narrowed her beady eyes at him when he hauled his gaze back to her, and he felt a warm sense of satisfaction inside. He had momentarily wondered if they were all snickering at his obvious discomfort, but their expressions seemed to suggest otherwise. It would appear that the rest of the party had the old witch's measure, too.

She looked down at a buff folder that was on the table in front of her and began rifling through a few pages.

"Mr. Fielding gave us permission to use this land for as long as we needed," she began. "We intend to trek up into the mountain the day after tomorrow—though I'm not sure yet how many horses we will need for that. Is there anywhere else around here where we can take some action shots? Nowhere filthy, mind you... Remember, we are trying to promote the clothes."

Kean fought back the urge to roll his eyes. This woman was in the middle of a field, planning a trip up the mountains, and here she was, worried about a little dirt.

"There's woodland over to the east a little if you don't mind a short walk, and if you want a more open aspect, the foothills run on for several miles just over there." He nodded to the far end of the marquee, indicating the direction, but Tabitha had already lost interest.

"Well, I've got an important meeting with Ms. Trotter in the morning. I'm hoping she will have more of an idea what sort of thing she's looking for — not that I suppose it matters too much for the local rag." She sighed, clearly finding the whole thing way too much trouble.

She wasn't the only one on that score. Kean had been horrified when he'd heard that *Country Girl* magazine wanted to do a photo shoot on Fielding land. He hadn't worked at the ranch for long, but he knew how particular the family was about their property — and with good reason. He was amazed that they'd agreed to all this in the first place — until he realized that the model they were using was Isla Gillingham. He'd seen pictures of her and had to admit she was a beauty — more so in real life, come to that. It would be good publicity for the ranch and they could never get too much of that. Trouble was…at what cost?

"The Fieldings had a meeting with Ms. Trotter earlier today and discussed her requirements, I believe, madam. I'm sure you'll be able to figure it all out when you see each other in the morning. In the meantime, I've been asked to check that you've got everythin' you need." Kean stared at the woman, silently daring her to make any demands of him.

She looked aghast at his revelation that his bosses had already organized the shoot with Ms. Trotter, and her face turned red and even tenser than before.

Talk about a bulldog chewin' a wasp!

There was a titter from Isla, who seemed to be enjoying the exchange, and he couldn't resist peeking over at her. She flushed at his attention. That surprised him, since she was a model, but he had to admit it made her look even prettier than ever.

His cock twitched and he shifted a little uncomfortably, while secretly admonishing his body for ratting on him. That girl had no place in his thoughts — or his feelings — and he was determined to remember that. She was lovely to look at it, but that didn't mean a thing. She was also a rich model and wouldn't want anything to do with the likes of him. He couldn't blame her, but he wished he didn't feel so damn disappointed about it.

"What time should I expect Mr. Fielding to grace us with his presence tomorrow?" Tabitha asked airily.

Kean seethed. She was clearly unhappy about being fobbed off with the hired hand instead of the boss, but it couldn't be helped. When he had gotten the message that both Fielding brothers had rushed over to the county hospital because their sister and her young son had been taken in after a car accident, there hadn't really been time to argue. Cordell Bray, the ranch foreman, had gone up the mountain to see to a problem with one of the horses, leaving him to take up the slack. Luckily, he'd been privy to arrangements about the shoot, so it made sense for him to come over and offer a little southern hospitality to the guests — even though he was from Northern Ireland. Besides, if he was ever going to have a chance at the assistant foreman's position, he was going to have to put himself out a little. He was already beginning to wonder whether this wasn't all a bit above and beyond the call of duty, though. This woman sure didn't like him, and he'd noticed that the bald guy hadn't introduced him to anyone else. No, he was clearly not cut out for this sort of role and everyone knew it.

"We're not certain yet, madam, but I'll ask someone to give you a call before they come over if you prefer — to make sure it's convenient for you?"

Tabitha's face went crimson and he knew she'd picked up on his sarcastic tone. He smiled at her as innocently as he could manage, and she narrowed her eyes, clearly seeing right through him, as was his intention.

Kean wasn't surprised to see her face tense up again as she must have been fighting the urge to question his manner, but she seemed to change her mind as she looked around to see her colleagues watching her.

"That would be most helpful." Her tone was clipped, making Kean grin even wider.

He nodded and casually replaced his hat. After a quick look around the rest of the party—particularly a certain young lady—he turned and left them.

It was bitter outside compared to the warmth of the marquee, and he pulled the collar of his Carhartt jacket around his neck as he strolled back over to his pickup.

He shook his head at the floodlights that had been left burning, while the rowdy generator roared across the countryside. Thank goodness these people were only planning to stay a week at the most. He didn't think he could bear all this upheaval any longer than that, and he was dang sure the local wildlife would feel the same way.

* * * *

Kean's mood hadn't improved much when he awoke the following morning. Somehow, his normal dreams about how he was going to get back onto his feet and repay his dad everything he owed had been intercepted by the gorgeous model from the marquee.

Isla Gillingham had smiled and giggled her way through his thoughts, leaving him waking to a squelchy wet patch on his sheets and a hard-on that could prop up the big top at one of his cousin's circuses. *Damn!*

The kettle boiled as he threw his sticky bedding into the washing machine along with the towel he had used for the shower. He shook his head as the motor ground and spluttered into action.

"Don't you be cutting out on me now," he urged the noisy machine as his laundry whirled slowly.

He had furnished his little shack with secondhand everything and was well aware that most of it wouldn't last long. The washer hadn't cost much, and he could see why. Every wash he put through it sounded as if it would be the last.

After making a cup of tea, he wandered over to the window. Despite the weatherman's claim that things were improving, he could detect snow in those thick clouds and shook his head at the thought. It was certainly getting colder, and Aidan Fielding had instructed them to start bringing the livestock down to lower ground yesterday. It wouldn't be long before the whole of Cavern County was whited out, being this close to the mountains.

He gave the washing machine one last look of warning before pulling on his prized possession, the battered brown Carhartt jacket he had bought at a charity shop, then headed outside. As he expected, it was bitterly cold and he was glad to have borrowed the firm's pickup again last night. He longed to get promoted so he could have full use of the vehicle and ease the three-mile trek to work every day. It was his choice to rent the old shack in the foothills, though, as the thought of sharing staff accommodation with a load of strangers really didn't appeal. He much preferred his own space.

He soon reached the Fielding Ranch and was reluctant to leave the warmth of the truck when he arrived.

The cowboy hat he wore as an attempt to fit in with the rest of the staff didn't offer much in the way of warmth, and he wished he could wear the woolly beanie he used to wear back home in Ireland. The jacket was warm, though, and the leather gloves preserved the life in his fingers. He was grateful for his beard, which he wore more for saving money on razor blades than for fashion, and his moustache, which afforded an extra layer of heat.

As he neared the staff hut—actually quite a salubrious building—he heard voices and stopped short at the mention of his name.

"What on earth possessed you to send Kean Maguire down as the welcoming committee?" Ben Fielding sounded quite annoyed.

Aiden, the younger brother, hooted with laughter.

"Come on, boss. He's okay," Cordell, the foreman, insisted. "I know his social skills aren't exactly his strongest asset, but he honestly was the best man for the job."

"Not his strongest asset? That's putting it mildly. I barely get more than a grunt out of the guy on a *good* day!" Ben sounded incredulous.

Kean's gut wrenched. He knew he wasn't the friendliest of people, but he hadn't realized that it was such an issue to his bosses. He'd never been particularly sociable or had a big circle of friends, but it was simply the way he was.

He felt like an outsider, an Irishman living in America. Everything was so much bigger here, brasher and stark. Back home, he had lived in a small town outside Belfast in the north of the country. His dad had moved him here when he had still been a teenager. Dad had remarried and Kean's new stepmom was from South Dakota. It was supposed to be a new start for the family — and boy, had Kean needed that.

"Top of the morning to you." If they were going to point out his failings, he'd damn well point out his differences. He nodded at each one in turn as he removed his hat, relishing the warmth of the staff kitchen.

Aiden grinned. "Morning, Kean. I hear you stepped up to the plate last night. Well done."

Cordell smiled at him, too, but Ben didn't look as happy.

"How did you get on with Ms. Merchant?" Ben seemed wary.

"Oh, Tabitha? Yeah, she was quite somethin'." Kean enjoyed the way Ben reared a little, his eyes wider and his face tightening by the second.

"Tell me you didn't call her by her first name." Ben's voice wasn't much above a whisper, to the delight of the Irishman.

Kean frowned. "I don't remember exactly," he said, as though thinking hard. "But it was all right. She didn't throw me out or anythin'. She was disappointed you weren't available to go in person, mind. I believe she's looking forward to meetin' you."

Ben glared at him. "What exactly did you say?"

Kean was enjoying winding up the boss and paused to

take the cup of coffee Cordell handed him.

"Thanks, boss." He nodded at the foreman, aware of the uneasy silence that had descended as they all waited to hear how last night had gone. "She said she's got a meetin' with that Ms. Trotter this morning. Is that her real name, by the way?" He frowned incredulously, shaking his head.

"Just get on with it." Ben was talking through gritted teeth and looked as if he would explode at any minute.

"Oh, right. Yes, of course. This Tabitha-woman's got a meetin' this morning, I think she said, with Ms. Trotter." He rolled his eyes at the woman's name, much to Ben's annoyance. "She'd like you to ring her before you go over there, to make sure she's free."

Kean enjoyed the way Ben's face tightened again, and Aiden and Cordell snickered.

"Would she now?"

"I hope that's all right. I didn't think you'd mind." He looked as innocently as he could, while Aiden chuckled.

"Seems like it'll have to be."

"She also said they want to go riding tomorrow and will need some horses. She didn't know how many, though. Oh, and they wanted some sort of woodland to take snaps in. I suggested Careless Copse. Is that okay with you?"

Ben raised his eyebrows.

The woodland had been given its nickname because of the number of horse-riding accidents that occurred there. Riders often enjoyed galloping their steeds over the meadows straight into the darkness of the dense trees. While the horses normally adapted quite well to the different terrain, it seemed a lot of riders were often taken by surprise by the dim light and low-hanging branches, resulting in a number of broken bones as they were swiped from their saddles.

"Good choice," Ben admitted.

"Won't it be a bit dark in there for taking photos?" Cordell frowned.

"They've got all sorts of floodlights and spots and stuff." Kean was instantly reminded of the racket those generators made. At least they wouldn't be bothered by the local wildlife with all that noise going on.

Cordell nodded. "Great. It's a lovely area for taking pictures, I'm sure they'll be pleased with that."

Kean immediately thought of the beautiful shots they could take of Isla Gillingham and he secretly admonished himself. He wished that woman would stay out of his head.

Chapter Three

Isla stretched, trying to get the knots out of her back. She was used to sleeping in the trailer but still longed for the luxury of her own bed. It had been a while since she had been home, although that wasn't necessarily such a bad thing. What used to be her sanctuary from all the mayhem had become a big problem — one she was glad to be away from. She shook her head, not wanting to think about that right now.

Her first outfit of the day was hanging in the tiny wardrobe and she smiled as she pulled on the soft denim jeans. She'd worn enough pairs of them to feel the difference in quality and these were one of the best she'd tried. The shirt was brushed cotton and she snuggled into it, glad of its weight as it was such a cold morning.

"Looking good," Alex remarked as she sat up in bed. "I knew it would."

"The shirt's a little big, but I like it." Isla smiled.

"I can always pin it a little if necessary, but it looks fine."

Isla cringed at the thought of using pins. They were often used to cinch in a waistline or alter a poorly cut garment, but she was always on edge when they were used near her skin. "I think it'll be okay."

Katie also shared the trailer, and Isla was surprised to see her bed empty.

"Surely it's way too cold for a run today." She shivered.

"You know Katie," Alex said with a roll of the eyes. "She's determined to lose another ten pounds before Christmas. Apparently, Tabitha told her she might have half a chance at a modeling career if she does."

Isla shook her head. "We'll have to find a way to talk her out of it. She really doesn't want to do this all day."

"*You* do." Alex got out of bed.

"Not one of my best choices," Isla told her, shaking her head. "There are plenty of times I wish I'd stuck with fashion design. I was stupid to listen to my boyfriend and I'd hate to see Katie make the same mistake."

"Yeah, I know. It was that Michael Danvers who first put this idea into her head. He even approached Tabitha to see what she thought. I couldn't believe it when Katie said she had to lose more weight, though. It's not as if she's big, is it?"

Isla sighed. Katie was a very pretty girl and certainly didn't need to get any thinner.

"I'll see you over there," Alex told her from the bathroom door.

Isla nodded as her stomach gurgled.

She pulled on the cowboy boots she needed to wear for the shoot, sighing at the feel of soft leather. It made such a nice change from the high heels she often had to wear, and she wriggled her toes at the luxury. She grabbed a jacket, already sensing the cold at the mere notion of leaving the snug trailer.

The ground was hard and she breathed in the fresh scent of the country. It took her back to her childhood and the ranch she had been brought up on with her grandparents. She'd loved helping out around the place and had even given riding lessons to the local children to bring in a little extra cash. She sure was looking forward to getting back in the saddle tomorrow, and she smiled as she made her way over the compacted soil to the big marquee.

The smell of pancakes welcomed her and she was surprised to see that Chad and Stefan were already up.

"Good morning beautiful." Stefan grinned. "Didn't expect to see you this early."

"I was thinking the same about you," Isla admitted, making her way over to the counter. It was good of Stefan to call her beautiful, seeing as she wasn't wearing any makeup yet and her hair was hanging a bit lifelessly around her shoulders.

"We want to go suss out the area for the shoot this morning," Stefan told her.

Isla smiled. Stefan was always well prepared and would only call her over to pose when he was sure everything was in place. Chad helped out with all the lifting and usually set up the lights with Stefan, as well as taking on most of the driving.

"That guy said it wasn't too far away," Isla remarked, trying to stop herself from smiling at the thought of 'that guy'.

Stefan smirked, obviously picking up on her expression. "Yeah. And what about 'that guy'?" He frowned thoughtfully as Isla joined them with her plate of pancakes. One of the reasons she liked to get up early was so she could eat without Tabitha passing comment on the number of calories she was consuming.

"Seemed like an odd one to me," Chad piped up.

"I thought he was quite nice." Isla hadn't intended to sound so defensive as the memory of the gorgeous cowboy returned to the place in her mind where it seemed to have taken residence ever since she had laid eyes on him.

Stefan snickered. "I knew you liked him. I saw how you were looking at him all the time he was talking to Tabitha."

Isla flushed and quickly busied herself eating breakfast.

"He handled her real well," Chad commented with a satisfied nod. "She didn't quite know what to make of him."

"None of us did"—Stefan rolled his eyes—"except perhaps Isla."

Again, she felt herself get hotter. "He was very polite."

"Polite? Holy cow, which cowboy were you looking at, girl?" Stefan teased her. "He was the most sullen, miserable cuss I've ever met. He almost didn't bother to speak to Tabitha at all. If he'd had his way, he'd have turned tail as soon as he arrived, I'll bet. Talk about looking for an excuse to back out."

Both men chuckled.

"He's got a point," Chad agreed when they'd recovered from their hysterics. "As soon as I spoke to him, he was looking back at that exit. He really didn't want to be here, did he?"

"Well, you didn't exactly welcome him with open arms," Isla pointed out indignantly. "Honestly, Chad, you could have introduced him to everyone. The poor guy must have felt like he was intruding or something."

"Yeah, Chad. How come you didn't introduce the hot cowboy to Isla? You must have known she was dying to meet him?" Stefan gaped sarcastically at him before both men roared with laughter.

Isla flushed again. "That's not what I meant, guys, and you know it. It would have been good manners, that's all."

"Sorry, Isla. You're right." Chad nodded, still chortling. "I didn't even get his name."

"Now there's the real crux of the matter," Stefan teased. "How can she crush on the guy when she doesn't even know his name? Come on, Chad. Do a girl a favor, why don't you?"

The men guffawed at this and Isla shot up with her empty plate.

"That's trash and you know it," she snapped at them before storming over to the counter where she plunked her plate down so heavily that she almost smashed it.

She stalked out of the marquee, glad they had been the only ones there but knowing the guys would soon be telling everyone about their crazy theory. And it was crazy, wasn't it? Why on earth would she have a crush on some sulky cowboy with a weird accent and a chip on his shoulder a mile high?

Isla hardly felt the cold as she strolled down the meadow. Her mind reeled with indignation and confusion. The guys were always teasing her. She really was used to it, so why did it bother her this much today? Could it have anything to do with the fact that they might be right? That handsome cowboy with the Irish lilt had been in her dreams all night and was still rattling around in her mind now. She'd been trying to guess what his name might be—Sean, maybe, or Declan. He was definitely Irish, not American-Irish, and she felt sure his name would be, too.

She hoped he hadn't noticed her expression when he came in and opened his mouth. The hat was completely at odds with his accent—and his manner. Most of the cowboys she knew were quite laid-back and most definitely American. This guy was a total enigma. A totally *gorgeous* enigma.

The grass felt crisp under her feet and the air was still and bitter. Fields surrounded her on three sides, with a blue mountain range on the other. Off in the distance, she could see what looked like a wooded area. That must have been where the Irish guy had suggested they do today's shoot.

She shivered. The cowboy hadn't looked at all happy to be there and clearly wasn't impressed with Tabitha's comment about him being the hired hand. Who would be? He wouldn't know that she was simply being her usual rude, condescending self. The way that tic had jerked in his neck was proof that the bitch had got to him, and Isla had actually been surprised that he hadn't retaliated. Using sarcasm had been the best way to deal with Tabitha, though, and boy, was he good at it.

She imagined he would be good at a lot of things. He sure was handsome—his short, wavy hair shining almost coppery in the stark lights of the marquee, his facial hair cut close to his skin in a neat and totally strokeable style. His eyes were dark and brooding, and he seemed to suck in everything around him in a controlled, measured fashion. That guy knew when they were snickering about what he'd said, and he was well aware of them staring at him. He wouldn't miss a trick. There was something calm and calculated about the way he had reacted to everyone, although she guessed he would have his volatile side, too. There was no getting away from the fact that she had studied the cowboy in miniscule detail and couldn't get him out of her mind — not that she really wanted to.

"Are you planning to wear your hair like that all day?" Alex stomped toward her, smiling.

Isla frowned.

"You've been out here for ages. We've had our breakfast and the guys are about to go scout out that area they're considering for the shoot. We need to get you ready or it'll be midnight before we get all set up."

She had no idea how long she'd been there, but it must have been a while if Alex's expression was anything to go by. Isla huffed and walked toward her. "Sorry. I was just thinking."

Alex gave her a knowing grin. She was a pretty brunette with bright green eyes and a round body. When she smiled, her whole face lit up and she was always joking about something. "Yeah, I guessed that much," she told her as they linked arms and trundled back toward the trailer.

Isla rolled her eyes, guessing the guys would have ratted on her already. She knew them so well.

"Come on then. Work some of your magic on me." Isla shook her head with a sigh as she climbed up the step.

"There you are." Katie looked as gorgeous as ever as she beamed over at them.

"Don't you start," Isla warned her, removing her jacket.

"My lips are sealed." Katie pulled her fingers in a zipping motion across her mouth and giggled. "Your secret's safe with both of us."

Isla frowned, taking her seat in front of the mirror. "What secret?"

"Didn't you know that you talk in your sleep?" Alex walked over with a comb in her hand and the flakiest innocent expression Isla had ever seen.

"What?" She went hot and her cheeks flushed as a memory suddenly haunted her. She always shared a trailer with the girls when they were on location and had woken one night after a nightmare. Alex had told her then that she had been

29

crying out in her sleep, but she had hoped it was just a one-off, brought on by the stress of something Tabitha had said.

Katie fixed a hair band on her before rubbing something cool and creamy onto her face. This would usually relax Isla and she would tip back her head to enjoy the sensations. Not today, though.

"It's true," Alex assured her airily, as she perched against the counter in front of Isla, pontificating while waving the comb around. "It wasn't anything bad, though, or we'd have woken you."

Katie giggled. "No. We got the impression you would want to stay asleep this time."

Isla felt as though her eyes would bulge out of her head. She could tell by the girls' expressions that they were being serious, even though they were obviously enjoying torturing her with the news. "What did I say?" She hardly dared ask.

"Well, there weren't any coherent words, exactly," Alex replied, "only murmurs and groans."

Isla swallowed as she recalled the thoughts that had swamped her dreams last night. *That dang cowboy.* On reflection, it was probably a good thing she hadn't gotten to know his name, as she would certainly have been screaming it out if she had.

* * * *

The shoot went very well and everyone was in high spirits by the time they broke for lunch.

"We'll be able to wrap this tomorrow, I'll bet," Stefan remarked, fiddling with one of his cameras while everyone sat around the big marquee.

Isla looked up from her salad, frowning. "Already?"

"Thank heavens for small mercies." Tabitha sat at the end of their table, shaking her head.

Stefan rolled his eyes. "Yeah, I should think so. We got some great shots this morning and if we go a little farther out, we can get some more this afternoon. Then I thought we'd take some tonight, maybe around dusk. Tomorrow, we'll head up into the mountain and take a few action shots and I think that'll be everything." He picked up the shooting schedule in front of him and nodded.

"Well, I met with Ben and Aiden Fielding this morning and they're happy for us to borrow a couple of horses," Tabitha informed them. "They're also going to lend us one of their staff as a guide. Apparently, it's a bit steep up there, even this far down, and they want to make sure you're safe."

Isla frowned indignantly. "I can ride, you know."

"You *used to* ride," Tabitha interjected. "It's got to have been a few years since you were on a horse."

"I'd have thought it was a bit like riding a bike. You never forget," Chad offered, lightening the mood a little.

"It'll be good to have some local knowledge. They should know the best places to take the photos," Stefan added, thoughtfully. "And if that guy who pointed out today's location has anything to do with it, we should get some great pics." He nodded, clearly impressed.

Isla felt a warm glow in her stomach at the thought of the cowboy who'd suggested the area for today's shoot. It had been the perfect location, with plenty of greenery as well as the backdrop of the mountains in the distance. She'd already seen some of Stefan's work and it looked amazing.

"If you think I'm asking for that ignorant man, you can think again!" Tabitha sneered. "As I told his bosses this morning, he was the most insolent person I've ever come across."

Isla shot to her feet, her heart hammering. "You told his bosses that? How could you? He might lose his job because of you."

Tabitha shrugged. "So? He obviously wasn't that happy to be here, was he? I've probably done them all a favor."

"You bitch!" Isla had never called her out before, but Tabitha had gone too far this time. "You don't care about anyone else but yourself." After throwing her napkin onto the table, she stormed out of the marquee, aware of the silence that had descended because of her outburst.

The air was cold but she welcomed its bite as she ran down the meadow. Since Tabitha Merchant had taken her on, she had tried her best to tolerate the woman's nasty remarks and attitude. Tabitha was a powerful woman and her contacts had helped Isla get some good jobs. But there was no denying she was also a grade-A bitch. The way she toyed with people's lives was unreal, and her sharp tongue could render the strongest person a jibbering wreck — men, as well as women.

Hot, angry tears rolled down her face, but she just kept running. It was all open fields around here, so she couldn't get lost, but she was determined to put some distance between her and Tabitha.

She came to a fence at the bottom of the field and leaned over it, burying her face in her hands. In the still, quiet air she bawled as loud as she wanted, content that no one could hear her while she got it all out of her system.

As she calmed down, she felt a little surprised at herself for reacting the way she had. It was unfair of Tabitha to berate the poor cowboy and possibly cost him his job, but there was more to this. She had never dared raise her voice to Tabitha before yesterday, and now she had done it again. She knew there was always a chance Tabitha would drop her like a hot potato, and once the bitch had gotten her teeth into her, she could make sure she never got another modeling job again. She had the contacts and the spite to do it. There were rumors that Tabitha had had something to do with the closure of one of the major magazines, *Beauty Personified*, although there was no evidence to confirm it — only that she had a lot of clout in the industry.

Somehow, the threat of losing her job didn't frighten Isla as much as it should have. She was becoming tired of having people preen her all the time — telling her what to wear, what to do, how to act — and that was without actually posing for the camera. Tabitha seemed to own her and she couldn't seem to escape her grip. If she wasn't a model, she didn't know what she'd do, but there had to be something. She sure couldn't go on like this.

Chapter Four

"Was everything all right last night?" Cordell's tone told Kean something clearly *wasn't*.

He frowned, sipping his coffee. "In what way?"

Cordell took the chair opposite him at the little table of the kitchenette. "Ben and Aiden went over to meet Tabitha Merchant earlier," he began, warily. "You didn't upset her or anything, did you?"

Kean racked his brain. "I explained that they were unavailable and that I had come to check that everything was okay. I asked if she needed anything. What did I miss?"

"You *were* polite to her, weren't you?"

"Of course." Kean's heart thumped harder as he wondered what the old witch had said about him.

Cordell studied his face, which was somewhat disarming, before nodding slowly. "Okay."

The thought rankled. "Did she say somethin'?"

"No, that's just it. Ben felt there was something she *wasn't* saying. I think maybe she found you a little...abrupt."

Kean shot his head up in surprise. That wasn't the word he was expecting to hear. He grinned. "She's obviously not used to the strong, silent type," he said. "I was there for business and that was all, not social chit-chat. Besides, it was late. They all looked tired. I didn't want to outstay me welcome, if you know what I mean."

Cordell snickered, shaking his head. "All right." He stood and put his cup in the sink before turning back to him. "They'll need a couple of horses for their trek up the mountain tomorrow. Think you can handle that?"

Kean nodded. "I'm sure I can manage it, boss."

Cordell narrowed his eyes at him. "They also need a guide to take them up."

A knot twisted in Kean's stomach as he slowly realized what the foreman was suggesting. He was hardly the right man for a job like that. Besides, he had thought that he would be the last person Tabitha Merchant would want to see, especially if she had found him a little — what was it? — *abrupt.* Ben wouldn't have chosen him for the job either, judging by what he'd said earlier.

He stared up at Cordell's questioning look. If he pulled this off, it would certainly show them all that he wasn't as sullen as they seemed to think. It might even give him a better chance at the assistant foreman's job he so badly needed. Pure devilment at seeing Tabitha's reaction twitched at his lips, and the thought of seeing Isla Gillingham again warmed his churning stomach.

Slowly he stood, still studying his boss's expression. "I know my way around that part of the mountain and I'm a skilled horseman," he said slowly. "I've already established a relationship with the client and now that we've brought the rest of the livestock to lower ground, you won't need as many hands to manage them. I reckon *I'd* be best placed leadin' the party on their shoot." His heartbeat almost deafened him as he waited for Cordell's reply, and he was relieved to see the grin that split his boss's face.

Ben walked in just as Cordell opened his mouth to speak. "It's good news," he announced. "Josie's going to be okay."

Cordell reached out his hand to shake Ben's, and Kean nodded his acknowledgment.

"Good to hear," Cordell said with a grin. "She had us all worried."

"Give her me regards." Kean's voice was quiet but both men turned and stared at him, their eyebrows almost disappearing into their hats.

"I will." Ben nodded appreciatively and Kean went hot with embarrassment.

Cordell had been right when he'd said that Josie's

accident had worried everyone. She'd been driving home when a truck with only one working headlight had pulled out in front of her. She had rammed right into it. As soon as they'd gotten the call, her brothers had rushed to the hospital where they had spent most of the night waiting for her to regain consciousness. Kean had been surprised at how much it had affected the whole staff, himself included. The Fielding brothers ran the thriving ranch extremely well and everyone who worked for them became a sort of extension of their family. Kean longed to fit in with them all, as everyone seemed very close and they certainly cared about each other. They might not care for him, though, if they knew all about him.

"Kean's going to arrange the horses for the photo shoot tomorrow and he'll take them up the mountain in the morning," Cordell said, gesturing toward him.

Ben's face fell slightly and it was clear he was trying to keep his shock under control. "Really?" He frowned.

"It'll be fine," Cordell assured him.

Ben gaped from Kean to Cordell before taking a deep breath. "It's your decision," he conceded. He glanced back at Kean. "It's only the photographer and the model. They're not doing anything technical."

Kean nodded, secretly enjoying the boss's discomfort with the situation.

Ben quickly shot back at Cordell. "Right. Well, I'll be off. Aiden's still at the hospital but I thought I'd better check how things were going here."

"We've brought all the livestock down," Cordell told him. "I reckon we're in for snow soon."

"Exactly what I was thinking." Ben raised his eyebrows, clearly impressed.

Kean grinned as the boss left. He was determined to see a lot more of that expression.

* * * *

The atmosphere between Isla and Tabitha was as bitter as the air outside, and they avoided each other as much as they could.

"I think she's expecting you to apologize," Alex confided as she, Katie and Isla sat at their own table for supper.

"Well, she can damn well think again." Isla was sick of knowing the woman's beady eyes bore into her back as she ate. "She had no right ruining someone's career like that."

"What about *your* career?" Alex murmured.

Isla's stomach jolted. She knew only too well that she could lose out if she antagonized Tabitha to the point of firing her, but it didn't bother her as much as she thought it would. She shrugged. Maybe it was time for a change.

The night shoot didn't take long, and Stefan was delighted with the results.

"It sure is beautiful out here," he remarked as they packed up his cameras and equipment.

"I don't think I could live in the country," Chad piped up. "There must be wolves and all sorts of wildlife out there. You honestly don't know what to expect."

"Like you do back home, you mean? There could be a madman around every corner. I believe I'd rather take my chances with a wolf." Stefan chuckled as he hoisted a bag onto his shoulder.

"I'm with Stefan," Isla said. "Give me animals over people any day."

The girls murmured their agreement.

"I could live out here," Katie told them wistfully, looking up at the clear sky. "It's so calm and tranquil."

"Me too. You can sense the peacefulness in the air. And look at all those stars. You don't see them like that in Sioux Falls." Isla gazed up as a million heavenly bodies twinkled down at her.

"But don't you think it might get a big boring, ladies? I mean, apart from stargazing and walking through dirt, what else is there to do around here?" Chad scorned playfully as they all trudged back over the meadow and toward the marquee.

"People do have jobs out here, you know, Chad." Isla frowned incredulously. "There is civilization — shops, offices, businesses. It's a much smaller scale and more relaxed than back home, though."

"Well, I wish we had a more relaxed atmosphere around here," Stefan murmured as they neared the outskirts of the area where they were pitched. "Tabitha's like a bear with a sore head. Can't you sort that out, darlin'? Do us all a favor."

Isla huffed. "How did this all become *my* fault?" Her voice was a little louder than she intended. "I was only sticking up for the guy. He didn't deserve to lose his job merely because Tabitha didn't like him."

"Oh, yeah, we're back to the cowboy again, are we?" Chad teased.

Isla flushed. "I simply don't think she was fair to him, okay?" she protested.

"And the fact that he was handsome had nothing to do with it, I suppose?" Chad went on.

"Well, you'd know. You had more to do with him than the rest of us," Isla snapped.

"You've got to admit he was rather hunky," Alex chirped.

"Was he? I can't say I noticed." Isla tried to say it airily but knew she'd failed to convince anyone.

"Methinks the lady doth protest too much." Stefan chuckled.

Isla's heart quickened as she tried to think of a cute comeback. "I was more interested in how rude Tabitha was to the stranger, to be honest. Was I the only one to see it?" She wondered if a slight change of subject might help.

It didn't.

"He was rather gorgeous," Katie piped up.

Isla shot her friend a glare. *I thought you were on my side here.*

Chad and Stefan burst out laughing, much to Isla's annoyance, and she kept quiet for the rest of the walk.

As Tabitha insisted on having a trailer all to herself, it was also used for storing most of the large equipment. Isla dreaded seeing the older woman when they went to drop off the lighting gear and the small generator.

As predicted, Tabitha sneered when she saw them outside the door and reluctantly let Stefan go inside. The others handed the equipment over to him and he stored it at one end of the vehicle.

"We'll take the rest over to ours," Chad told him after offloading the largest items, and they all turned to go.

"Thank you, Tabitha. That's extremely kind of you. Sorry to have disturbed you, Tabitha," the older woman sniped sarcastically and Isla felt her blood boil.

Spinning around to face her, she literally bit her tongue as she caught the satisfied smirk on Tabitha's face. That was what she wanted — an all-out row. Why was she deliberately trying to provoke a reaction?

Isla glared at her but was determined not to give the bitch the satisfaction she craved. Instead, she would treat that remark with the contempt it deserved. Sticking her nose in the air, she followed the others back to the other trailer, her heart pattering like tribal drums while her body shook with angry frustration.

The good thing about encountering Tabitha in the trailer was that they knew she wouldn't be in the marquee when they all piled in for a warm drink after having put away the rest of the gear.

"I don't know what her problem is," Isla groaned as they all nursed their cocoa. "She's gotten ten times worse lately."

"Marvelous Models might be closing down," Katie told her matter-of-factly. "Tabitha's recently lost the contract with that magazine she was working with, *Blitz*, so they haven't got enough work. Some of the bigger names had already left anyhow, as soon as the news was leaked, and Tabitha's been tearing her hair out. That's probably why she's been such a bitch lately."

Isla gaped at her friend. Marvelous Models was the

flagship of the Merchant Models enterprise. Tabitha had fingers in a lot of pies, and had bought up several small and failing companies. Although her methods were usually ruthless, her business acumen was second to none. For her to lose any of her firms would be devastating, but Marvelous Models was absolutely tragic.

"How do you know all this?" Isla gasped.

"Yeah, and how come we didn't?" Alex chipped in.

Katie gave them a smug smile. "I overheard her talking on the phone the other day, so I did some digging on the Internet. She's lost loads of money recently, and Tessa Rose and Poppy Vinton leaving has caused an avalanche of backlash. A lot of other models are talking about pulling out now that those two have gone. It looks like that's how she lost the *Blitz* contract."

Stefan whistled, shaking his head.

"*Blitz* was worth a fortune to her," Alex cooed. "It wasn't just the money. The kudos pulled in a load of other clients. If she's lost that, she may well lose more of her agencies."

Isla huffed. With Tessa and Poppy gone, she was one of the biggest names on Tabitha's books. No wonder she'd been so annoyed at the thought of Isla doing this job for nothing. The firm's expenses were being paid, therefore Tabitha wasn't losing out on it, per se, and Isla had already paid her the commission she would have earned had it been a paid job, albeit at a reduced rate.

"Still want to get into modeling?" she asked Katie.

The redhead pouted. "I'm merely thinking about it."

"It's hardly a stable business," Alex said.

"What is these days?" Chad pointed out. "I mean, look how *Beauty Personified* suddenly folded — and we still don't know how it happened. There's something not right there. I heard its finances are being investigated for fraud after a shedload of money went missing. This sure isn't the industry it used to be."

"I don't think I'll be in it much longer anyway," Isla confided.

Stefan stood to get another drink. "She won't fire you. You're the best she's got, darlin'."

"No, I don't mean that. It's just... I've had enough, you know? Everyone's so catty, and the backbiting gets me down. Tabitha's a total bitch and doesn't mind who she walks over to get what she wants. I'm tired. Tired of walking on egg shells around inflated egos. Tired of being told what to do all the time. Tired of living out of a suitcase."

Her last statement brought back a vision of the apartment she shared with Verity Sanders back in Sioux Falls. It was in a neat building and they'd furnished it beautifully. Unfortunately, Verity's boyfriend, Wayne Warrens, seemed to have taken up permanent residence there, too. It wasn't a problem while Isla was working away. It was nice for Verity not to be left alone all the time. But he stayed there when she was home, too, and his presence wasn't a welcome one. He had made numerous passes at Isla and often muttered lewd comments when Verity couldn't hear. Despite telling him in no uncertain terms that she wasn't interested, Isla didn't seem to be able to convince him. The situation was even worse because Verity was such a lovely friend, and Isla couldn't bear to upset her by telling her what a rat she was dating. She'd decided that the best thing she could do was take all the jobs she could, anything to keep out of the apartment. Even if she stayed on Tabitha's books, it looked like the work was going to dry up anyhow. She couldn't win.

"You'd actually leave?" Chad looked agog.

"I thought you were only venting," Katie admitted, her face turning pale.

Isla shook her head, her short curls caressing her cheeks. "No, I mean it. I'm not happy doing this anymore. I mean, I love being with you guys, of course, but I feel like it's time I found something else. You know?"

"I hope you pick your moment to tell Tabitha that," Stefan remarked.

"Don't worry. I will." Isla smiled nervously.

Chapter Five

Kean woke up surprisingly early the next morning with a massive hard-on and a smile on his face. The wet patch next to him just proved that the woman who was on his mind had clearly been there all night. *Damn.* Any more of this and he'd have to buy more bedding.

He dragged himself into the shower and tugged at his hard cock while supporting himself with one hand against the cool wall tiles. Visions of Isla Gillingham's dazzling smile flashed through his mind — her licking her full lips, inviting him to plant tiny kisses on them before he plunged his tongue into her mouth, exploring and owning every inch of it. Her big, hazel gaze would stare into his eyes, making his cock burn with need. He would nibble his way down her long neck and slip his tongue into the delicious hollow at its base, before meandering down to her pert, full breasts that he would delight in nipping and sucking while she moaned uncontrollably.

The cock in his hand ached painfully as he rubbed it fiercely from root to tip, gently squeezing as he went.

In his mind, he would trail his hands all over Isla's perfect body — touching, caressing and loving every inch. She would groan at his ministrations and open her legs fully, offering him her glistening pussy. He would first enjoy her with his mouth, lapping at the juices that would trail endlessly down her soft lips. She would twitch as he slowly licked her perineum and right up to the tiny nub that would cause her to scream, begging for more.

The hot cream of pre-cum began to drip down his fingers at the mere thought, and he was glad of the warm shower to wash it away.

He imagined Isla's gasp as he would eventually introduce her pussy to his cock, teasing her with soft nudges at her entrance before plunging balls-deep inside her warmth. She would yell out in fervent ecstasy, thrashing her head from side to side, clawing at his flesh as he would pump in and out of her welcoming depths. Her uncontrollable groans would spur him on and he would thrust harder and harder as she would scream wildly for more until they would climax together with feral, earsplitting cries before he slumped down beside her, his need for her closeness surpassing his need for air.

He roared as his juices spurted like a geyser up the wall of the shower cubicle, relief burning through his body before he crouched down under the warm stream of water. His legs had buckled beneath him and he panted hard in an attempt to recover.

After a leisurely scrub, he trimmed his beard before dressing in a clean shirt and jeans. He chuckled at himself as he fueled up on copious cups of tea. *When was the last time a girl had this effect on me?* If it had ever happened, he couldn't remember it. There was just something about Isla Gillingham.

He already had an emergency pack together, along with first aid, plenty of water and a packed lunch. He wasn't too sure how long they were planning to be up on the mountain, but it was better to be safe than sorry.

He had snagged the work pickup again and whistled as he drove down to the ranch.

Cordell had already gotten one of the hands to saddle up the horses for him, and he grinned as he mounted.

"Got everything you need?" Cordell looked slightly amused, and Kean guessed it was because he thought Kean would be well out of his comfort zone.

"Yes, sir."

"Have you seen the weather warnings? Snow's on the way. You be careful up there, ya hear?"

"I heard it. Not due for a while yet, though. We should be okay."

"Well, good luck." Cordell stood back.

Kean nodded. He hoped he was conveying a confidence about his job rather than delight at seeing the beautiful model again, and he waved to the boss as he rode out, leading the two extra horses.

When he arrived at the field where the photographic team had set up camp, he was surprised to see that they appeared to be packing up some of their belongings. A thud landed in his stomach, wondering whether they had changed their mind about the shoot and decided to go home. His initial disappointment was replaced by annoyance at the thought that they hadn't bothered to inform the ranch — or him — of their change of plan.

"What the hell are you doing here?"

Kean turned his head at the screech. Tabitha Merchant stepped down from one of the trailers. Her eyes seemed to be on stalks and her mouth was still in the constant sneer he remembered from the other night.

He carefully dismounted and walked toward her, the tic in his neck suddenly working overtime. He tipped his hat politely. There was no way she would be able to tell his bosses that he was rude.

"Good morning, madam. I've come to take some members of your party up into the mountains. I understand they have arranged a photo shoot today."

"They sent *you*?"

"Yes, madam." Kean relished the look of horror on her face and smiled sweetly at her, just to increase her pain.

"Hi there."

The young, good-looking guy from the other night walked over to them, and Kean couldn't be sure whether it was a smile or a smirk on his tanned, clean-shaven face.

"Are you taking us for the shoot?"

Kean nodded, forcing himself to smile. "Yes, sir."

"Great. I'm Stefan Randall, the photographer. Isla's just

getting her things together." He reached out for Kean's hand, his shake firmer than the cowboy expected.

"I wasn't sure if you'd changed your mind." Kean gestured to Chad, who was carrying a large box out of the marquee and toward one of the other trailers.

"Nah, not a chance." Stefan grinned. "We're looking forward to it. We move out this afternoon, though. I heard there's snow on the way, so we wanted to get moving as soon as the shoot's over. They're packing away so we're ready to roll once we're back."

Kean was surprised at how relieved he felt.

"I take it you won't be too long." Tabitha's sharp voice reminded him of her presence.

"Well, I guess that depends on what pictures I can get, Tabitha. Sometimes everything lines up right and other times it takes a while. You know how these things work." Stefan definitely smirked this time.

"I've got three locations in mind, but obviously, it's entirely up to you." Kean leaned toward Stefan. "There's a stream at the foot of the mountain, then a little farther up there's a ledge where you'll get a magnificent view of the whole valley on a day like this. If there's time, I can take you up to the waterfall, but that depends on the weather. Snow's not due till later on, but you never can tell up there." He nodded toward the mountain.

"Well, that sounds perfect." Stefan smiled with a nod of approval.

"I'd better see what's keeping Isla," Tabitha grumbled, leaving them.

She hadn't gotten far when Isla came running out of a trailer, looking flushed. She stopped short when she caught up to them and stared at Kean. "It's you."

He felt a little uneasy, trying to gauge her expression. *Is that good or bad?* She didn't look as horrified as Tabitha had, but she sure looked astonished to see him.

"Yes, miss. Mr. Fielding sent me over to act as your guide up the mountain today. Is that okay with you?" His voice was a little defensive.

Isla gasped. "Yes. Yes, of course. It's just that…" She looked questioningly at Tabitha who had followed her. The older woman rolled her eyes, shaking her head.

Isla looked back at Kean with a dazzling smile that lit the whole of her face. "That's fantastic," she assured him, nodding.

Kean nodded back. It was all he could do. He couldn't possibly speak right then. Her beauty captivated him, while her reaction confused him, and his memory of her from this morning's shower embarrassed him half to death.

"Have you got everything?" Tabitha snapped.

Kean cleared his throat hurriedly. "I've got blankets and plenty of water but you'll need an extra sweater and a cell, if nothin' else."

"Be back in a sec," Stefan promised before he and Isla rushed back to the trailers.

"I hope you know what you're doing."

Kean turned to Tabitha, struggling not to roll his eyes. "I'm sorry, madam. Were you talking to me?" He frowned.

She looked a little taken aback. "Yes, of course I was. I said that I hope you know what you're doing up there. Mountains can be dangerous places. Are you qualified to take a couple of inexperienced riders up there with the threat of snow on the way? What if something happens? Isla's insurers will be suing you for incompetence, you understand. She's a very important asset to my company and I can't afford for her to be off work because of your negligence."

Taking a deep breath, Kean shook his head. "The weather isn't expected to deteriorate until later this evening, by which time you'll be well on your way. And Mr. Fielding informed me that both riders *are* experienced. If that's not the case…"

"They may have ridden before. I don't remember. I only know that they're not as used to all this as you are. You need to make sure they're kept safe, no matter what. Isla has a very proactive legal team who will not only sue your ass off, but they may also shut down the ranch altogether. She's not a woman to be taken lightly, you know?" Tabitha's voice was becoming more and more shrill.

Kean sighed. She obviously didn't trust him, and that explained Isla's earlier reaction, too. No one thought he was up to the job. Tabitha was obviously expecting something to go wrong and he would get all the blame, regardless of what it was. If Isla's legal eagles were as sharp as the older woman was making out, they would find something to hang on him, whatever happened.

He got that Isla Gillingham was a beautiful model, but by the way Tabitha was talking, it seemed she was an absolute diva. She would be watching his every move, just looking for something to sue his sorry ass for. It was how the rich got richer anyhow, wasn't it?

Disappointment smothered him at the realization that the girl who he made love to in his dream wasn't the girl he was taking on this trip. He stared at the ground, giving it a self-deprecating smile. Of course, she wasn't going to be like that. *What was I thinking?* He had known before he'd met her that she would be some attention-seeking bitch who was simply out to make a quick buck where she could. Well, he hated to disappoint a lady, but he was damned if he intended to be her next meal ticket.

* * * *

Isla gazed at the beautiful countryside all around them as they ventured up into the foothills of the craggy, blue mountains. She was glad she'd put on an extra sweater as the air was getting colder, though not as cold as the atmosphere between the little party as they rode in virtual silence.

"Is it far to the stream?" Stefan asked.

"No."

The sullen cowboy had offered nothing but one-word

answers and grunts ever since they'd left camp, and it was beginning to drive Isla insane. She was sure he had been in a better mood than this when she'd first seen him this morning, but ever since they had begun their venture up here, he had been as miserable as sin.

"It's good of you to be our guide today." She hoped a little soft-soap might help.

"Hmm."

It didn't.

She was in the middle with him in front and Stefan bringing up the rear. She turned to look behind her.

"Isn't this gorgeous? Think we can get some good shots today?" She tried to sound cheerful.

Stefan nodded. "Definitely."

A few minutes later they saw the stream up ahead. It twinkled in the winter sun, splashing over the rocks and down the mountain. They stopped the horses and dismounted.

"This is lovely," she gushed, trying to provoke a positive reaction from their guide.

"I haven't brought a lot of equipment, so we're relying on the sunlight and natural shadows. Let's try you over by the tree to start with. I'm hoping a little dappled shade might be quite effective." Stefan sprang into action, measuring the light and changing the lens in his camera.

Isla quickly pulled a comb through her curls and checked her makeup in her compact mirror, aware of the disapproving expression on Kean's tense face. She shook her head. *I'm a model, for fuck's sake. Get over it.*

"Beautiful, darlin'." Stefan snapped away at her ever-changing poses. "Something a bit more natural now. Don't look at the camera. Just move about and I'll click as and when."

It embarrassed Isla, knowing that Kean was watching them. She ran a hand down the bark of the tree, her face tilted up to the sunlight. Then she walked over to the stream and placed her fingers in the cold water. She sighed, wishing she could go to places like this all the time. She missed the country and was only living in Sioux Falls for the convenience of work. It wasn't often she got assignments like this, not that she really wanted to take any more modeling jobs anyway. If she could spend all her time riding up mountains and toying with silver streams, she would in a heartbeat. There was a warm sense of belonging here.

"Look out!"

She had been so lost in her thoughts that she had forgotten what she was doing, and suddenly slipped in the wet mud of the grass verge. Stefan had shouted, but it was Kean who ran forward and caught her just in time. His body was hard and warm as he pulled her toward him, and he stood as firm as a rock.

"Oh." Instinctively, she threw her arms around his neck, knocking his hat into the dirt. She found his hair with one hand and twisted it in her fingers while holding on to him for dear life with the other.

His manly fragrance engulfed her senses and she was a little dazed as she stared up at him. His dark eyes were as brooding as the rest of him and it seemed like he could see right into her soul. His initial look of alarm had dissipated and he now appeared concerned, worried. He blinked with a swallow and suddenly his expression was blank, unreadable. He held an air of confidence that eased her panic, and she gasped as she drank him in.

Kean moved forward until she could feel his breath on her neck. Her heart pounded.

"You need to be more careful." His voice was deep and permeated her core.

Isla balked as her panties began getting wet and she immediately squeezed her thighs together in embarrassment.

The cowboy let out a low chuckle before leading her away from the bank of the stream. He held her close to his body and she shivered with nerves as they walked.

"Wow, that was close!" Stefan shook his head as they neared him.

Kean still had a strong arm around her and she didn't want him to remove it—ever. She felt safe having him so close, and his warmth and spicy scent surrounded her.

"Are you okay?" Stefan frowned.

"Yeah, I-I just lost my footing for a moment." Her face heated.

"I was so busy taking pictures that I hadn't noticed how close you'd gotten to the edge." Stefan gave a self-deprecating smile. "It's a good job Kean was here." He nodded at the cowboy who removed his arm from around her.

Isla looked up at him—big mistake. He was gorgeous, his big dark eyes studying her carefully, toying with his tongue on his bottom lip.

She took a deep breath, forcing herself to pull away from his magnetism for a moment. "Thank you," she whispered. "You saved me."

Kean let out an incredulous laugh. "From what? Getting your feet wet? There's barely a foot of water in the deepest part and you were nowhere near that," he scorned.

Stefan chuckled. "Well, at least it saved having to change your boots. Come on. Let's get to the next location. I'm getting cold standing here."

Isla's stomach churned and sickness threatened the back of her throat. She had been genuinely concerned for a moment there, and she thought Kean had been, too. It seemed she was totally wrong about him. As her face flushed at their reactions, she quickly made her way to her horse. The sooner she was out of here, the better.

Chapter Six

The atmosphere hung around them like a thick cloak as they made their way farther up the mountain. Kean knew she wasn't happy, but there was nothing he could do about it.

When they'd set off from the stream, Isla had tried to change places with Stefan, but Kean had put his foot down.

"I've got strict orders to keep you safe," he'd growled at her. "That's a lot easier if you stick close to me."

He had noticed the way her eyes had widened and he knew she liked that idea more than she was prepared to admit. Then her face had tightened and she nodded, as though something had just clicked into place in that pretty little head of hers. Now she was giving him the cold shoulder — which wasn't hard. It was freezing up here.

"I think that snow might be here a little sooner than we thought," he told them, looking up at the heavy sky. "We might not get as far as the waterfall, but we'll get to that beauty spot I was tellin' you about. It might be a little slippery on the ledge, though, so you need to be extra careful, okay?"

"I hear ya," Stefan piped up.

When Isla didn't reply, he turned to her.

"Did you hear what I said?" His voice was clipped.

She narrowed her eyes as she stared at him. "Yes, I did."

Hmm, she is certainly mad at me over something. "And are you capable of taking care of yourself up there or should we turn back now?" He stopped his horse.

She pursed her lips angrily, letting out a long breath, obviously while she considered her response. He didn't mind. He could sit there all day if he had to, looking at that beautiful face.

His thoughts wandered back to the feel of her in his arms earlier. Her slender frame had molded into his body perfectly and he relished her closeness and the heady scent of that expensive perfume she wore. He'd been worried sick at first that she was actually going to fall into the stream. Despite his claims that the water wasn't that deep, there were sharp rocks under there that could cause untold damage to that pretty face of hers, if nothing else. Seeing the panic in her eyes had sobered him, though, and he hoped he'd shown her that he was competent enough to keep her safe. He hadn't wanted to let go of her, and when he'd whispered in her ear, he'd had to force himself not to kiss her soft skin.

Kean knew he shouldn't have ridiculed her like that, but he had to do something to change the mood. It was all getting a little intense, and with that other guy hanging around, he could hardly accept her adulation, now could he? And he was still trying to suss out whether the photographer was actually her boyfriend or not. He sure seemed worried about her.

"Yes." She was staring at him defiantly, and he'd almost forgotten he'd asked her a question.

"Good. Then we best get on before the weather turns on us." With that, he tugged on the reins and led them up the ridge.

Isla shivered as they rode up the narrow mountain track. The air was icy and she was glad she'd worn extra clothing for the trip. She watched Kean's tall frame as he sat perfectly upright on his horse, glancing back at her and Stefan every now and then but not speaking. He sure was handsome, but she was a little sick of his moods. When he had caught her earlier, she had imagined for a second that they had shared a moment of mutual understanding – of attraction, even. Now she could see that she'd gotten it all wrong. Kean

Maguire was simply toying with her, stringing her along so he could make fun of her. Well, if he thought she was going to get upset over it, he could damn well think again. He had no right making her look stupid. He was their guide. He was being paid to bring them up here and make sure they were safe, not to belittle them.

Flooded with indignation and embarrassment, she stuck her nose in the air. "Will it take long to get to the next destination?"

Kean looked back at her in surprise. "About ten minutes more by me reckoning. You in a hurry?"

"Yeah. I merely want to get this over and done with so we can all get going. Everyone's waiting for us to get back before we can go home. I don't want to keep them." She raised her eyebrows airily. If he wanted to show that he was in charge of the trip then that was fine, but with that responsibility, he would also be culpable for their time-keeping.

"When were you planning to finish taking your pictures?" he asked.

"There's no rush," Stefan called from behind her. *Damn.*

"Really?" Kean looked doubtfully at Isla, making her squirm. "I thought you were worried about not getting back to your camp on time, not that I was ever given a time frame to work on in the first place. Maybe you should have mentioned your other plans before we arranged this trip so I could ensure we kept to your schedule."

She swallowed hard, knowing he was right.

"We're not working to a schedule," Stefan called over, frowning. "We just want to take the best photos we can then get back. If it's a problem for the others, they can always head home in Tabitha's trailer. One of the rigs, too, if they all want to go. Chad's not in a rush to go. He'll wait to take us."

"So, there're all sitting around waiting for you to finish?" Kean looked incredulous.

"No, they're going up to the ranch this morning to see

your bosses. Tabitha's got a meeting booked at half past ten. The catering guys usually take a few hours to get everything packed up and ready to roll, then Stewart, Joe and Frank need to take down the marquee. Joe and Frank are the other drivers anyhow, so no one can go anywhere until they're done." Stefan grinned. "If you ask me, we've got the best job today. I vote we take as long as we like. It's all hands on deck once they start pulling down the poles for the marquee. I know where I'd rather be."

Kean narrowed his eyes, focusing his attention on Isla. "So, it's only you who wants to get back then, eh?"

She flushed, seething at his knowing expression.

"I don't believe in leaving all the work to everyone else," she protested. "It's not fair to them. It's me who agreed to do the shoot, after all."

"Correction... It's you who agreed to do it all for *free*, darlin'," Stefan interjected. "The rest of us are quite happy to eek this out as long as it takes. We all get paid, even if you don't. This is our livelihood, don't forget. If you end the shoot early, we could lose money. No, I think we're doing them a favor being up here, if you ask me."

"I wasn't," Isla muttered angrily under her breath.

Kean smirked at her and she looked away, biting her tongue. Trust Stefan not to back her up. He might be a flirt when he was working, but he was certainly one of the boys when he wasn't. The guys chuckled and she knew they were laughing at her, but there was nothing she could say. She pulled her coat around her a little tighter and stared right ahead.

The path got narrower as they rode on, and her heart beat a little faster at how steep it was becoming.

"Right around this next bend the track widens out and there's a ledge where we can dismount," Kean told them. "We leave the horses there and make our way on foot to the next ledge, where you'll see the magnificent view I was telling you about. We can grab something to eat while we're there, too — unless, of course, you don't have the time?" He looked pointedly at Isla and she heard Stefan sniggering behind her.

"Let's get on with it, shall we?" she snapped.

Although Kean turned back around to face the way they were heading, she could tell by his posture that he was having a quiet chortle at her expense. She tensed. It sure wasn't the enjoyable day's riding she had been hoping for.

"This is it." Kean slid elegantly from his horse and she was surprised at how quickly he was standing next to hers, a hand out ready to help her down. She would have thought him quite chivalrous had it not been for his previous quips — or the smug look on his face.

She didn't hold his hand but made a point of climbing down — not quite as gracefully as she'd have liked — then brushed past him as she hit the ground. The low chuckle that emanated from the back of his throat irritated the hell out of her but she was damned if she was going to retaliate.

Grabbing a water bottle from her saddlebag along with the little purse that contained her comb and lipstick, she felt his eyes boring into her. Despite her best efforts not to, she glanced up to see his amused expression as he stood, arms folded, watching her.

"What?" she spat the word out at him.

He shrugged. "Just let me know when you're ready," he said, airily. "I've got all the time in the world. Although, it might be better if we were on lower ground before it gets dark, especially as it definitely looks like snow's on the way. Don't let me rush you, though, madam — all in your own good time." He held up his hand to her, emphasizing his devil-may-care attitude, and his eyes twinkled with mirth.

Isla huffed. "I was only grabbing a couple of things," she mumbled. She was totally irked that he had called her 'madam', although she'd found it quite funny when he'd called Tabitha that. It obviously wasn't a word that came naturally to him, and she guessed it would have sounded even more stupid had he used the colloquial 'ma'am'.

"Everything all right?" Stefan eyed them both warily.

Kean threw her a questioning glance.

"Of course," she replied curtly. "Why wouldn't it be?"

The men exchanged a look that did nothing to improve Isla's mood and she followed them across to where the ledge narrowed to a single track. The cold wind bit her as she carefully negotiated the rocky terrain, aware of Kean's constant checking on her. She would have been flattered had she not been so damn annoyed.

Isla was more relieved than she cared to admit when the track widened again and they found themselves on what seemed like a large shelf, cut away in the side of the mountain. It was the first time she'd dared to peer out over the side and the view took her breath away. She could see for miles over the tops of trees, out to far-reaching farms and ranches way off in the distance. Grassland spread like a large green tablecloth over the undulating foothills and flat terrain, while cattle and horses appeared more like ants from up here.

Stefan whistled his approval as he followed her gaze.

"I promised you a view," Kean remarked proudly.

Isla rolled her eyes. *I suppose this is all you're doing, is it? You laid all this on especially for us, did you? Talk about a high opinion of yourself... You think you created all this!*

She was surprised on glancing over at him to see the hurt look on his face. *Maybe he can read minds, too.* She quickly turned away and pulled out her compact and comb, afraid that her expression may have given away her thoughts.

"This is beautiful," Stefan said, pulling his camera from his rucksack.

"I hope it's light enough for you," Kean replied, frowning up at the sky.

What will you do if it's not, turn the sun back on? Isla shook her head at the thought. Being so mean, even if only inside her head, didn't make her feel at all good about herself. He truly was a handsome guy, and he'd done quite well to pick out these locations for them, but he was just utterly infuriating.

"It'll be fine for what we want," Stefan assured him, "and, besides, I've always got this." He held up a long, thin telescopic pole that had a large, battery-operated light on the end.

Kean nodded. "I'll hold it for you, if you like."

Isla was surprised at his offer but said nothing. It seemed it was only *her* he was being an asshole with.

They were soon set up and Isla actually felt nervous about posing in front of both of them. Kean's eyes never seemed to leave her, although he was very adept at holding the lamp in position for Stefan, who continued to make his usual murmurs of encouragement.

She was happier once she'd gotten into her stride and forgot about the camera and its crew while she looked out over the gorgeous countryside. The air was still and quiet while the sky was thick with unshed snowflakes. They weren't as high as she'd initially thought, as the foothills rolled for miles into the distance, and she felt a little easier knowing that she was safer than she'd imagined.

"Okay, now look over your shoulder then straight into the camera, flicking your hair as you bring your head around," Stefan instructed.

She did as he asked and enjoyed his coos of appreciation. "That's great, darlin' — and again."

She had her right arm leaning against the rock face as she swung her head over her left shoulder then whizzed it around to the front again, intending to smile right down the lens. This time, though, she felt dizzy and misjudged the distance between her face and the hard rock next to it. Her scream pierced the tranquility as agony shot through her head and down her cheek. Everything went blurry and she sank to the ground in a haze of confusion and pain.

"Isla." She heard Kean's broad accent as he ran over to her, dropping the lamp with a clatter in his hurry to help. He wrapped his strong arms around her shoulders as she held her head in her hands and he crouched down. He took a clean handkerchief from his pocket and dabbed at the blood before taking her hand and positioning it to keep the fabric in place.

Surrounded in his warmth and safety, she took a second to gather her thoughts before a frantic yell made them both look up. With a scuffle of rock dust, Stefan tripped over the light and fell backward over the steep ledge.

Isla screamed in horror while everything seemed to happen in slow motion. Kean left her on the ground, her heartbeat threatening to deafen her, as he ran over to where Stefan had been. He was already on his cell, calling out mountain rescue for help, diligently reeling off their exact whereabouts in a calm, competent manner.

Tears streamed down Isla's face as she slowly stood and made her way over to him.

"Stay where you are." Kean's order was abrupt.

Isla balked, frozen to the spot while he continued his conversation with the control office, as though he hadn't just yelled at her. Her vision had cleared and she felt stupid and ashamed for crying out like that. She had no idea whether Stefan was okay or not, but the fact that Kean wasn't shouting down to him was a bad sign.

After what seemed like forever but was probably only a few minutes, Kean slipped the cell back into his pocket and turned back to her. "Don't come over here," he told her, his voice deep and quiet.

Her whole body went hot and she stared at him, mortified.

He held up a hand, as though reading her thoughts. "It's all right. He's probably knocked himself out. He hasn't fallen that far down."

She let out a long breath. "Knocked himself out?" Her voice wasn't much above a whisper as relief swept through her.

"Yeah. Seems to be a lot of it going around."

She glared at him as fury swamped her bones. Her anger increased as he shook his head dismissively at her and peered over the side of the cliff again. Although desperate to yell at him, Isla could see that their priority was Stefan right now, not some petty row, even if it had been brewing all day.

Kean looked up into the murky sky. "They'll be sending a helicopter out," he announced. "You need to get back over to the side of the rock and crouch down as low as you can. Take shelter behind that boulder there. See?"

She looked to where he was pointing and nodded.

"Do it now," he instructed.

He sounded so dominant that she daren't argue and quickly went to where he'd indicated.

"Get down on the ground," he called over to her. "The down draft'll sweep you right off the ledge if you're not careful."

She gaped at him and immediately did as he'd said.

"Good. Now I'm going back to calm the horses. They'll panic once the chopper gets close and might try to bolt. Can I trust you to stay there and not move?"

Isla was disappointed that he wasn't going to wait with her, then she promptly admonished herself for thinking that way.

"Yes."

"Good. Your man's not going anywhere, so don't be tempted to come take a look, okay? There's nothing to see anyhow."

Isla was about to tell him Stefan wasn't 'her man' then realized that it was actually his Irish turn of phrase. She loved his accent and could listen to it all day. *Or all night.* Once again she chided herself for that thought, trying to remember how annoyed she was with the way he had treated her.

She gaped at him as he made his way over to the narrow track and she was sad when he disappeared from sight. The mountain suddenly seemed very lonely and quiet. The thought of Stefan down the cliff somewhere, hurt and unconscious, ate at her heart. It was her fault. If she hadn't made a fuss about hitting her goddam face, none of this would have happened. Kean wouldn't have dropped the lamp and come running, and Stefan would be safe now, probably calling a wrap on the day's shoot. *How could I have been so stupid?*

The *whop-whop* of the helicopter dragged her thoughts back and she looked up to see it getting nearer. She felt as though she should be out there, standing on the ledge, pointing to where Stefan lay, but she couldn't move. Not only was she afraid that she would only make things worse, but she also remembered what Kean had said. The downdraft was getting stronger as it neared the edge of the mountain, and she froze with the cold.

The helicopter circled an area not far from where she was crouched, and she realized that Stefan must have been quite close to the rock. Despite her fascination with how they would get down to where the casualty lay, she had to screw her eyes tightly as rock dust was blown into them, and she buried her head in her arms while holding on to the boulder for dear life.

The sound of the helicopter was deafening and she hummed to herself to try to drown out the noise as well as the fear. She wasn't sure how long she crouched there, slowly rocking back and forth while concentrating on the sound of her own voice in an attempt to block out everything going on around her.

Suddenly something tapped her shoulder and she yelped as she jumped, her whole body tensing to a solid mass as a stranger stood next to her.

Chapter Seven

"Hey, it's okay. My name's Mike Forster."

A man in a thick, green coverall stood over her, smiling.

Isla swallowed hard, blinking profusely.

"I heard you bashed your face. Mind if I take a look?" He removed his helmet and pulled out a small pack strapped to his waist.

"It's okay. I'm fine," she murmured, not quite sure what was going on. "It's Stefan that's hurt."

"The guy who fell over the edge?" He was having to shout over the din of the helicopter, although it sounded a little farther away than before.

She nodded.

"Is he your friend?"

"Yeah. He's the photographer."

"He's going to be okay. Looks like a concussion. Might have broken a leg, too. We're taking him back to get checked out properly, but it doesn't look too bad. I just wanted to make sure we didn't need to take you along, too. Your friend on the phone was real worried about you." Mike was wearing plastic gloves as he gently wiped a swab over her forehead and down her cheek.

Isla stared at him as his words permeated her brain. *Kean was worried about me?*

"You'll live," Mike announced with a grin. "You've grazed your cheek quite badly and you'll have a heck of a bruise in an hour or two—but nothing drastic. You might need to take some Advil once the headache really hits, but you don't need to come in."

Isla nodded gratefully as he radioed back to the air

ambulance.

"Stay down there. Your friend's coming back for you once we're out of your hair," he told her with a grin. He put his helmet back on after fastening the first-aid pack around his waist.

The noise of the helicopter rose again and she shielded her eyes from the dust as she saw it moving a little closer to the ledge. A long ladder descended from its open door and Mike reached out, attached himself to a safety rope and caught a rung before signaling to his colleagues.

"Thank you." Isla wasn't sure whether he heard her as she called over to him, and she watched in awe as he was winched up into the moving aircraft.

She sighed with relief as the helicopter became a tiny black dot in the distance and only then did she venture out from behind the rock. She stretched then shivered with cold. Frowning, she realized that it had started snowing already and the ledge was covered in a thin white blanket.

The broken lamp was almost covered, and she could just make out Stefan's camera as the dim sunlight caught the lens.

"Don't even think about it," a familiar voice growled to her and she shot her head around to see Kean walking toward her.

"What?" She frowned.

"You know full well what. You were going to head over to the edge there and retrieve the camera."

"Well, we can't possibly leave it there. It's worth thousands." She stared at him incredulously.

"Money isn't everything in life, you know," he informed her, piously. "And, besides, I thought I told you to stay put." He shook his head, making her feel like a naughty schoolgirl, and he went over to pick up the camera. "It's already quite slippery," he went on, "and we don't want any more accidents, do we?"

She huffed at his superior attitude, his tone really grating on her nerves. "Meaning?" she demanded, folding her arms.

He raised his eyebrows. "Meaning we don't want any more accidents," he repeated.

"You mean you don't want me to *cause* any more accidents," she accused him, frowning. "You think this is all *my* fault, don't you?"

Kean looked at her then up at the sky. "This snow's not going to stop any time soon and it'll be getting dark shortly," he said. "We need to get back to the horses and walk them down as far as the lower ground. We can't risk riding them up here in this."

She stared at him as though he were an alien. He was completely ignoring what she'd said.

"That means we haven't got time to waste," he said firmly. "Come on."

Despite wanting to stand and argue the point, she knew it made sense to follow him, so she stuck her nose in the air again and trudged along behind him as they carefully and slowly made their way along the narrow track to where the horses stood patiently waiting.

Isla seethed all the way back down the mountain trail, while Kean seemed to delight in warning her of slippery areas and crumbling rock.

She walked behind with her horse as he led the other two. She had to admit that he was a skilled horseman and certainly seemed to know his stuff. Not only was he gorgeous, but he was perfectly competent, too. *Damn him!*

"We can ride from here," he announced when they reached flatter ground.

Isla shuddered. It was cold enough as it was without adding the extra altitude to the equation, but she would be glad to get back to camp quicker, so she hoisted herself into the saddle.

The horses' hooves thudded in the thick snow and she was amazed at how quickly it had deepened. She frowned.

"I need to call Tabitha. She should be told about Stefan and warned that I'm going to be late getting back. They should have set off already. It'll take ages to get home in this."

Kean shook his head. "Don't worry about it. She knows everything."

She narrowed her eyes at him, her cell phone still in her shivering hand. "What?"

"Don't you think they might have worried when they saw the air rescue helicopter over here? I rang ages ago to let her and the Fieldings know what was going on."

She went hot. *She* should have been the one to tell Tabitha, not him. She looked around at the snow-laden trees and miles of whiteness that spread out in front of them. "Hold on... We're going the wrong way." An air of self-satisfaction washed over her at the thought that he'd made a mistake. It was short lived, however.

"We're not goin' back to the camp. It's too far and too late. Your friends have left already. There was no way they could hang around waiting for the weather to worsen with a five-hour journey in front of them." They were riding side by side now and he seemed to be studying her reaction.

Isla swallowed hard. "They've gone without me? All of them?" A lump stuck in her throat at the thought of being abandoned.

"It was the safest thing to do," he said.

"But how will I get home?" Her heart pounded painfully against her ribs. She didn't have her car and there was no way she could catch a train all the way out here. Her face became hotter and imminent tears gathered behind her eyes, much like lemmings on a cliff edge.

"They'll send a car when the weather improves. You can stay with me until then. It's not far." Kean sounded very matter-of-fact as he dropped his bombshell on her.

She gasped. The snow was still coming down thick and fast and she knew the roads would be murder, but surely there was an alternative to staying with him?

"So, we're going to the Fielding Ranch, I presume?" She tried to keep the tremble out of her voice. Surely the

Fielding brothers would offer her a room there. She was a client, after all.

"Nah, it's too far and the horses shouldn't try to cross the river in this." He looked upward. The sky was dark gray and heavy. It was getting late.

Her stomach churned. She had no other option than to accept his hospitality. The warm feeling inside her when she thought about her predicament seemed to belie her outward disdain at the idea, and she quickly turned away as she heard Kean's deep chuckle.

* * * *

Kean opened the door to his little shack and let her in. He gulped, wondering what a girl like her would make of how he lived, but they didn't really have much choice in the matter.

"Make yourself at home. I'll go see to the horses," he told her and headed over to the rundown outbuildings that stood nearby.

The wind had sprung up and the snow almost blinded him as he led the three horses over, and he was glad to open the large wooden door and let them in out of the cold. Being sheltered from the weather immediately made him a little warmer, although he was looking forward to being able to feel his fingers and toes again sometime soon. He quickly unsaddled them as they helped themselves to the hay that had been left there. Some oats were stored in a large sack at the back and he quickly poured them into a couple of buckets.

The water had frozen in its large container, and the faucet had iced over. He picked up a couple of spare buckets and took a deep breath before opening the door and bracing the cold flurry of snow again.

He trudged back to the house and was glad to see that Isla had put on a couple of lights. The heat hit him as soon as he got inside, and he was welcomed with the smell of fresh coffee.

"Is everything okay?" Isla called through from the tiny living room.

He gaped when he peered in and saw that she had already lit the fire. She smiled at him, replacing the fire guard. She had removed her coat, hat and boots and seemed quite cozy in her warm sweater and jeans.

Kean smiled at her thick, fluffy socks. "I just need to get some water," he announced, holding up the buckets.

"I boiled the kettle in case you needed it," she offered, following him through to the kitchen. "And there's coffee. I hope you don't mind. I thought..."

"It's fine," he assured her, noticing her concern. "In fact, it's grand." He nodded, surprised to see how well she seemed to fit in his home.

"It appears to be getting worse," she remarked, looking out the window while he filled the buckets.

"I reckon it's in for a day or two. We've got enough supplies to last, though, so it's nothing to worry about." He heaved the buckets out of the sink and toward the back door. "I won't be long."

"Be careful." Her eyes were big and beseeching as she held the door open for him, and he was surprised at her concern.

"Don't worry. I'll be fine."

He snagged a couple of old blankets and shuddered as he faced the blizzard again, screwing up his eyes as he took the pails over to the shed. The horses seemed oblivious to the conditions as they munched happily at their feed and he plunked down the buckets for them before covering the animals with the blankets.

The snow reached his knees as he went back to the house and he looked forward to warming himself in front of that roaring fire. He was impressed that Isla had managed to light it, having assumed she was much more used to central heating than log fires.

He'd almost reached the house when his foot slipped and

he fell headlong into a pile of soft snow. Immediately, he heard the back door open and Isla called out to him.

"Kean, are you all right?"

He quickly snapped up his head, annoyed at making a fool of himself in front of her. "I'm grand. You stay there."

After getting to his feet, he shook himself down before looking over at her. When he did, his heart lurched.

Isla stood in the kitchen doorway with a large steaming mug of coffee in one hand and a thick blanket in the other. She had been waiting for his return and must have been watching for him, judging by the speed at which she'd pounced when he'd fallen.

"Come on," she urged as a wide smile split her face.

For a second Kean wished she could live here with him all the time, as this was a scene he would love to relive — even the falling down part. He smiled back at her, no longer feeling the cold, and tramped toward the open door.

He removed his hat and immediately began to peel away his coat before taking a sip of the hot coffee. He kicked off his boots as Isla wrapped the warm blanket around his shoulders.

"You must have sprung a leak!" Isla pointed at the ice that covered his socks.

"Yeah." He didn't want to tell her that he already knew he had holes in his boots as they were second-hand, but they were all he could afford right now. "I'll go change. You should get some dry pants on, too. Come on. I'll get you a pair."

She said nothing but followed him to his bedroom where the bed lay unmade and a small pile of laundry had gathered in one corner. Kean balked, wishing he had merely offered to bring her out a pair of Levi's, but it was too late now.

"Sorry 'bout the mess." For the first time, he was actually glad that the light bulb was quite dim, but he studied her face as she looked around.

"You should see mine," she replied with a smile.

That wasn't the reaction he had expected and he felt

instantly relieved by it. This girl sure was full of surprises.

He went over to his closet and pulled out a pair of jeans, some lounge pants and a couple of sweaters.

"Don't forget your socks," she reminded him, still standing in the doorway.

He rolled his eyes. "You sound like me mam."

Isla giggled. He loved the sound—a sort of tinkling, almost like bells ringing. She looked even prettier now that she wasn't scowling at him, too.

He pulled a pair of thick woolen socks from his drawer and held them up for her approval.

She rewarded him with a satisfied nod.

"Do you need any?"

She shook her head. "No, thanks. Mine are fine."

He shut the drawer again. It had been a daft question, really. There was no way Isla Gillingham would walk around with tears in her boots. He sighed at the massive difference between them and went back over to where he had laid the clothes on his bed. After taking up the lounge pants and a sweater, he offered them to her. "I hope these aren't too big. You can change in here if you like. I'll take the bathroom. I could use a shower anyhow."

"Thanks."

He was a little nervous leaving her alone to nose around his bedroom, but he badly needed to get out of his wet clothes. Falling had soaked him to the bone and he knew he would catch a chill if he waited any longer. He drank the rest of his coffee while undressing, then hopped into the shower.

The hot water seeped into his soul and he closed his eyes to savor the luxury. His muscles relaxed and his aching body eased as he languished in the warmth. It had been a long day and he would be glad to get to sleep tonight. He frowned at the sudden realization.

I only have one bed.

Chapter Eight

After dinner, they sat in the cozy living room in front of a roaring fire.

"This is lovely," Isla said with a smile.

Kean sighed. "I'm sure it's not what you're used to."

"Ha. I wish it was."

Kean frowned, seemingly taken aback by her reply. "What? You'd rather live in a drafty old shack in the middle of nowhere instead of your penthouse apartment with central heating and all the modern conveniences? Yeah, right."

Isla looked over to him, raising her eyebrows. He was sitting in what she assumed would be his usual chair while she had the sofa to one side of him. "What on earth made you think I'd live in a penthouse?"

He shrugged. "Well, near enough, I'd imagine. You must be on good money. Maggie Fielding reckons you've had some really top jobs in your career. You're obviously doing all right for yourself."

She narrowed her eyes at him. They'd had a lovely meal, but she had sensed a slight uncertainty about him. She had hoped he would be much more relaxed after a warm shower, but he had seemed a little on edge ever since he'd emerged from the bathroom.

"I live in an apartment with central heating," she agreed, "but it's hardly state-of-the-art, and it's not mine. I'm living with a friend. The place is hers."

Kean looked surprised. He pouted. "I assumed you'd have your own place."

"I was planning to get one somewhere," she said, with a

sigh. "I'd been living with my boyfriend, Rob, for a couple of years, but when we split, I moved out. Verity offered to put me up for a while, so I moved in with her and her guy, Terry. Not long after that, she found he'd been unfaithful and she dumped him. We consoled each other. I didn't want to move out and leave her on her own. She seemed totally lost without Terry." She shrugged. "She got over it, though, and soon found someone else — Wayne. He makes me nervous. He started spending more and more time around the apartment, so I took more jobs on location. I've been hoping to move out soon, especially now. I don't want Verity to feel offended, though." She stared into the dancing flames.

"Why now?"

She looked over at him again, shaking her head. "What?"

He was studying her curiously and she searched her brain for a reason why.

"You said you were hoping to move out soon, especially now. Why now?" He frowned.

Isla's cheeks went hot and she swallowed hard. She hadn't meant to say that. "Oh, I just think it's time." She shrugged, quickly averting her gaze back to the fire.

She was surprised to hear him grunt, and she knew he didn't believe her. She couldn't go into detail, though. *What will he think?*

"Do you have the number for the hospital?" She decided a change of subject was in order. "I want to check on Stefan."

Kean nodded and stood up. "I'll get it. It's in my phone." He fetched his cell from the sideboard. "What's your number? I'll send it over," he offered.

Warmth filled her at the thought of them swapping cell numbers, even if it was only for practical reasons. She quickly saved his before making the call.

She was pleased when the sister told her that Stefan was absolutely fine and was sitting up in bed flirting with the nurses.

"So, he'll be out tomorrow?" she asked eagerly.

"If not, then the day after," the sister informed.

"That's great news. Thank you very much." Isla was relieved, still feeling guilty about the accident.

"He's okay," she told Kean, as though he hadn't just sat there and listened to her conversation anyhow.

"That's good." He nodded.

"They might let him out tomorrow, but I don't know how he'll get home," she said with a frown. "You said the crew had all gone back, didn't you? Will they send a car for us, do you think?"

Kean shook his head. "I doubt it. This weather looks set in for at least a day or two. I'd be surprised if anything's moving until it eases up."

She stared at him, her heart hammering. "You mean, we could be stranded here?"

Kean raised his eyebrows. "I'm sorry if the conditions aren't up to your standard, but at least you're warm and dry here. It could be much worse, you know."

Isla's blood ran cold as she realized what she'd said. "Oh no, I didn't mean it like that," she said quickly. "It's merely the thought of being cut off, not able to go anywhere—not able to get home."

"A few minutes ago you were saying you were plannin' to move out of your place. How come it suddenly seems so much more appealin' now than being here? Am I that bad?" He actually looked offended and she felt sick for sounding ungrateful.

"I'm sorry. I didn't mean—"

"Forget it." He put up a hand to halt her words as he stood again. "I get the picture. You can have my bed tonight. Tomorrow, I'll see if there's any way of gettin' you across to the ranch. You might be more comfortable with the Fieldings. They're filthy rich. I'm sure you'll fit right in there." He walked out and slammed the living room door.

Isla wanted the ground to swallow her. It had all come out wrong.

Kean returned a few minutes later with a handful of

blankets that he plunked on the chair he'd been sitting in.

"I'm quite happy to have the sofa," she mumbled. "I don't want to put you out."

"It's all right. I've changed the sheets if that's what's worrying you," he assured her.

"I didn't mean it like that and you damn well know it!" She shot to her feet, tired of not being able to say the right thing.

"Do I? I don't know anythin'. I'm only a stupid Irish cowboy."

"Stop playing the victim here, Kean. It doesn't suit you. I didn't mean those things the way you took them at all. You're being way too sensitive." She shook her head at him.

"You remember one thing, princess," he said with a sneer. "You brought all this on yourself."

"And what the hell is that supposed to mean? I'm responsible for the weather now, am I?" She waved her hand in the air, her voice raising another octave.

"We wouldn't have been up there when the weather turned if it hadn't been for Stefan fallin' off the damn ledge. And we all know how that happened." He was clearly riled now, as he raised his voice, pointing at her.

"Oh, I see. That was *my* fault!"

"Well, if you hadn't made such a damn fuss about your 'accident' then *maybe* he wouldn't have jumped — then *maybe* he wouldn't have fallen off the edge of the fucking cliff!" Kean hollered at her, using air quotes for the word 'accident'.

She stared at him, horrified. "You...you think I pretended to hurt myself? Why on earth would I do that?"

"Oh, I don't know. Maybe so you could claim that I'd been negligent in my duties. I'm sure you'd get a lot of money out of suing the Fieldings. They are loaded, after all, and they've got their reputation to protect. Of course, I'd lose my job over it, but, hey, why would that bother you?" He sounded sarcastic as he huffed at her.

"What *are* you talking about?" She couldn't compute his

words.

"Oh, don't worry. I know how these things work, princess," he told her with a sneer. "Now why don't you go and get yourself some sleep — unless, of course, there's a pea under the mattress!"

Isla shook her head, finally realizing what he meant. "How dare you?" Her voice was much quieter as she gaped at him, mortified. "How dare you speak to me like that?"

Hot tears burned the back of her eyes as she made her way toward the door.

"Sleep tight, princess," he called after her in a mocking tone.

Without another word, Isla went to the warm kitchen, took her clothes from the rack where they had been drying next to the oven and made her way to the bathroom. After changing, she grabbed her cell and quietly let herself out of the house.

The cold wind whipped her face as it howled around the sides of the tiny building and she shivered. Snow was still pouring down and she struggled to put one foot in front of the other.

"What the hell are you playin' at now?" Kean's booming voice hollered at her from the front door.

She turned to see him hopping on one leg as he pulled on his boots before rushing out after her. He hadn't even stopped for a coat.

"Are you mad or just stupid?" he demanded.

"Fuck off, Kean! Leave me alone!"

"Why? So you can go out there and kill yourself, you mean? Oh no, princess. I'm not gettin' the blame for this one. You get that pretty little arse of yours back in the house right now. Do you hear me?"

"Or what?" she screamed at him, although the wind seemed to steal the words from her mouth.

"Or this."

She squealed as he grabbed her and hoisted her over his broad shoulder. His grip was tight as he carried her back into the house and slammed the door behind them. A cocktail of anger, indignation and shock ran though her as she hammered on his back and yelled at him to put her down.

Once inside, he slowly lowered her to the floor where she stared up into his eyes, her heart thumping madly against her ribs while she panted hard. She was shocked to see how wild his own eyes were as they gazed down at her, and her stomach lurched like she had never experienced before. Anger was suddenly forgotten, and in its place was something much more powerful.

Suddenly he wrapped his arms around her and crashed his lips hard against hers. He invaded her mouth with his tongue and she ran her fingers through his short, wavy hair, scraping her nails against his scalp.

She couldn't breathe. Heck, she couldn't think. He filled her mind with a fervent lust, the likes of which she'd never experienced, and she squealed into his mouth as he hoisted her gently into his arms and carried her into the bedroom.

The bed dipped softly beneath her and still his mouth held her captive. His warmth surrounded her when his hard body lay over hers, and she heard the thump as he kicked off his boots.

His kisses became more tender as he nibbled his way around her lips before making a trail down her neck.

"I don't think you'll be needin' this," he growled, tugging at her coat.

Isla smiled and sat up slightly to allow him to remove it, and she, too, kicked off her boots.

"I guess you'll need to get those socks off, too," she said with a grin. "You'll catch your death of cold with wet feet."

He snickered and reached down with one hand to remove the soggy material.

"I think it's only fair that yours come off, too," he teased.

"No." Isla immediately tried to pull her knees up to her chest, giggling as she tried to elude his big hands.

Kean let out a laugh. "You're not just a wee bit ticklish

by any chance, now are you?" He grabbed her ankle and quickly ripped off one of her thick, pink fluffy socks. He ran his finger up the sole of her foot while she yelped, bucking backward.

"Kean, no!" She laughed loudly as he continued to torment her.

"Oh, now I've found your weakness." He clearly delighted in pulling off the other sock and tickling both her feet while she writhed and squirmed beneath him.

Isla giggled and whooped as he teased her, shivers running through her body.

"How about this then?" He bent down and took her big toe in his mouth, sucking hard and licking at it.

"Oh my God!" she screamed as a totally different sensation ran through her whole body. His breath was hot and his tongue was soft and thick as he laved affection on her toe, his eyes twinkling back at her. He licked her other toes, holding her foot firmly in his strong hand.

"Kean, don't!" She yelped, astounded by the shivers he was sending through her, horrified that he could make her feel this way with only her feet.

Her pussy ached, though she knew it didn't make sense, and hot juice escaped her as ripples of pleasure coursed through her.

She stared up at him as he tormented each toe, between each toe, under each toe. With a gasp, she screwed her eyes shut, realizing that he knew full well what he was doing to her — and how much she was loving it.

Her body stiffened, her nipples like bullets and her pussy clenched tight as she tried to ignore its constant throb.

Eventually he stopped with a deep chuckle, and she quickly opened her eyes as the bed dipped next to her. He lay over her now, and his erection dug into her, assuring her that she wasn't the only one affected by his ministrations.

"Kean," she whispered.

"Shh." He smothered her mouth once more and she inwardly sighed as his soothing tongue gently lapped at her seam until she opened up to him again. His kiss was tender this time, sensual and warm.

She hummed with delight, closing her eyes as she lost herself in his attention. He smelled fresh and his neat stubble grazed against her skin. He was all man. Gently he caressed her face while his kisses continued to soothe her. Isla floated on a warm thermal, sighing into his mouth as their tongues danced deliciously.

He ran his hands through her hair, tickled her cheek and trailed kisses around to her left ear. Biting gently on the lobe, he sent new sensations zinging through her body. He licked at her shell with his competent tongue while his teeth nipped all around it, causing her to shudder with heated pleasure.

She opened her eyes and gazed straight up at him. Kean's twinkled back with mischief and promise, while his dark brown irises had turned almost black with lust. She had never seen anyone so beautiful.

He raised one eyebrow, silently asking her permission before hauling his damp sweater over his head. Isla licked her lips instinctively. She was bereft at his brief loss of contact as he sat up to remove it, and she gazed hopefully at his black T-shirt.

Kean smirked and pulled the material from his torso. He was tan and ripped, and his chest bore a smattering of black hair. She gasped at the sight, feeling hotter by the second.

"Shall I?" His voice was low and gravelly as he tugged at the hem of her sweater.

Isla took a deep breath, desperate to be divested of the garment but unnerved at the effect his body was having on hers. In the two and a half years she had been with Rob, her longest-running boyfriend, she had never been anywhere near this turned on. She nodded slowly.

Kean smiled, leaning forward to pull the sweater up her heated body. Isla sat forward, relieved at the waft of cool air that surrounded her as soon as the woolen weight was removed from her flesh. Underneath it she wore a long-sleeved cotton top that was open at the neck where a line of four tiny buttons lay undone. He cocked that sexy eyebrow again and she nodded.

This time he touched her skin with rough fingers as he slowly stroked her waist while taking hold of the fabric. His gaze never left hers as he carefully pulled the top up her body and over her head.

He glanced down and smiled appreciatively at her breasts that seemed to be jutting toward him, begging for attention. The hard nubs of her nipples bulged through the satin of her bra and her chest heaved in anticipation.

Slowly, Kean leaned forward and ran a finger down her cheek. He kissed her lips softly, his hot breath enveloping her in an aura of assurance and hope. She reached her arms around his muscular neck, stroking the little hairs that curled into his nape. His weight descended over her, flesh on flesh as their chests met, hearts beating in time to the same deafening rhythm.

Chapter Nine

Kean tangled his fingers in her soft, blonde curls. He stroked the smooth skin of her neck, causing her to buck deliciously toward him with a soft moan.

He had never felt anything like it. It was like running his fingers through velvet. Her shoulders were like silk, and he couldn't resist trailing one hand down her body. She was extremely sensitive and jerked violently as he caressed her skin. He grinned. He'd remember that. The way she had reacted to his teasing with her feet had surprised and delighted him, and it was good to know her whole body was a mass of nerves, waiting to be teased mercilessly — and he was just the man for the job.

Isla arched her back, pushing her gorgeous breasts hard into his chest. He watched her face, her eyes fluttering open and closed all the time as she writhed beneath him. God, she was hot!

His rock-solid erection jabbed into her softness as it strained against the denim of his jeans, desperate for its release — desperate for her.

Kean kissed her again and she groaned into his mouth. She dug her fingers into the back of his neck and clung to him for dear life. They fought wildly with their tongues as their rampant breathing filled his ears.

Isla grappled at his waistband, her need surpassing her manners, and he loved it. She slid her slim fingers between his skin and the button that she quickly unfastened, and he sighed inwardly as she tugged at the metal zipper that was wedged against his erection.

With a deep chuckle, he slipped his own hand between

their groins, chancing a brief stroke over her pussy while he was there. Her breath hitched. *Good.*

She caressed his fingers as he yanked hard on the zipper, and she covered his hand with hers as he slid it down, freeing his desperate cock. Staring into her face for a reaction, he was relieved at the way she licked her lips, panting hard. Her eyes were on fire, pleading with him, and he didn't need asking twice.

Kneeling backward, he pulled the denim down his thighs then quickly stood as he hauled the jeans off his legs. The cooler air wafted across his skin and he welcomed it like a long-lost friend. His whole body felt like a furnace and he longed to divest himself of the last scrap of fabric that clung to his groin like a wet rag.

Isla was watching him, biting her lip, her chest heaving up and down as she panted. Her hands were at her waistband and he watched her unfasten her belt then the button. As she reached for her zipper, he took a step toward her.

"My job, I think."

She stared up at him, her eyes full of hope.

Kean grinned, running a finger over the denim that covered her pussy.

"Please," she whispered.

He nodded and slowly pulled at the zipper. Her whole body felt tense to his touch as he took the waistband and gently hauled the fabric from her and threw it next to his own jeans.

Her legs were smooth and freshly waxed. Her pink satin panties were plastered to her pussy in a dark, sticky mass of passion. He watched her chest heaving and she stared at him, full of desire. She raised one knee, sliding her foot slowly up the bed and put her arms above her head, offering herself to him, while at the same time teasing him.

His cock twitched at the sight and she licked those full lips of hers again. The ache in his groin told him he couldn't wait much longer and he hoped that the look in her eye was telling him she felt the same.

Although desperate to jump on top of her, to feel her skin once more, he couldn't resist gazing at her beauty for one more minute. She posed beautifully and he wondered if she had ever had photos taken in only her underwear — or less. If she had, he would love to see the results, although he would be jealous of the photographer who had shot them. He wondered if it would have been Stefan. His earlier concerns about them being an item had dissipated when they had been up on the mountain taking pictures. The camera loved her, but Stefan didn't. He flirted with her, but Kean could tell that there was no real emotion between them. And he would know. He had scrutinized her every move, every expression.

"Kean?" Her voice was smooth, like melted chocolate, and he suddenly realized he was staring at her.

His cock reacted to her before the rest of him. He smiled and she visibly relaxed. Slowly, he kneeled on the bed. Isla reached out her hand to him and he took it in his. Her skin was like the satin of her underwear.

Gazing at her gorgeous face, he gently kissed the tips of her fingers before trailing them down his torso and planting them on the waistband of his briefs. She gasped with surprise but took hold of the elastic, still staring back into his eyes. Carefully, she peeled the fabric from his body, allowing his cock to spring free of its confines.

Relief washed through him and he gasped at the sensation. Isla continued to pull the sodden fabric down his legs, still watching only his face. He helped her remove his briefs then took her fingers and placed them around his throbbing member. Only then did she look down.

Kean was certainly well-endowed and she gazed at his stiff cock that seemed way too big for her small hand. It was warm and hard, oozing passion and need. She ran her hand up and down his shaft, feeling the veins beneath her fingers and the desperation in his tension. Kean panted hard, his whole body seeming to judder.

With a gentle tug, she urged him to get nearer, and he followed her lead. He reached down and grazed a hand over the satin of her bra, causing her nipples to harden even more, trying to thrust themselves into his grasp. He snickered and knelt next to her.

His proximity caused the scent of his arousal to waft over her and she licked her lips as his manhood edged nearer to her. He moved back a little, however, to throw her bra over his shoulder and she shivered as the cool air surrounded her liberated breasts.

"Beautiful," he murmured, staring at her body.

Isla swallowed hard. In her line of work, she was used to people telling her how good she looked, but when Kean said it, it meant something — everything.

She closed her eyes as he reached forward again and fondled the soft flesh of her left breast. The slight coarseness of his fingers felt good against the aching need of her skin, and she relished the purchase. He caressed her right breast with his other hand, and again the bed dipped as he neared to her a little more.

She still had her hand wrapped firmly around his cock, and it twitched under her touch. She relished the effect her body was evidently having on his and pushed her breasts farther into his grasp. His deep chuckle told her that he knew exactly what she was doing and she opened her eyes to judge his reaction. He was gazing down at her with hooded eyes, his body rigid and proud. He swung a leg over her so he was now kneeling astride her, watching her expression as he did so.

Isla sighed at the warmth of his legs next to her hips and sank into the bed a little more. She was perched on a knife edge, awaiting his next move. He was taking his time, squeezing and caressing her breasts, the glint in his eye telling her he knew exactly what he was doing.

Her pussy ached and another spurt of hot liquid soaked her already-sodden panties. His cock was like a rod of iron in her hand and she quickened her pace as she ran it up and down from root to tip.

Kean moaned, closing his eyes. She'd hit the right spot. She continued in a steady rhythm, feeling him twitch and jerk beneath her fingers. His body began to sway in time to her ministrations and he was starting to lose control.

Her panties became even wetter as they stuck uncomfortably to her skin and she longed for him to take them off. As if reading her thoughts, Kean suddenly opened his eyes and grabbed the soggy satin with both hands. The loss of his fingers on her breasts was compensated by the relief of finally getting rid of her underwear. She quickly drew up her knee and swung her leg over him to ease the release of the panties, which he tossed onto the floor.

She quickly slipped her other leg around him and was rewarded with the touch of his heated cock against the smooth flesh of her pussy. Her body was waxed to within an inch of its life, which she usually found a nuisance to keep up, but the closeness of his skin next to hers suddenly made it all worthwhile.

"Please." Her voice was breathy as she pleaded with him, but he placed his hand firmly over hers, holding his cock still.

"Are you sure?" His eyes were as black as night and seemed to pierce her soul as she stared up at him.

"Yes. Please, Kean, I want this."

He leaned over to the night stand and opened the drawer. He pulled out a foil packet, then returned his attention to her.

"Please." She longed for this more than anything in the world. His throbbing body had tormented her long enough. She would burst if he didn't take her now.

After opening the packet with his teeth, he swiftly sheathed himself, still not peeling his eyes from hers.

He leaned over her, one hand on her shoulder, his chest hair tickling her breasts and his cock nudging at her swollen pussy. She opened her legs a little wider, feeling his flesh against hers. She wanted to suck him into her, to swallow that huge cock and own it—own him—but she couldn't. She had to wait for him. This was his decision, too.

A split second later he had decided. He allowed his heaving cock to nudge her entrance. Bracing herself for his sheer enormity, she willed her muscles to relax while widening her legs even more.

He was gentle, not forceful. He was slow, deliberate. He was perfect.

She stared into his eyes as he entered her, forcing her channel to expand in order to accommodate his girth. The sensation was unbelievable. Isla had never experienced anything like it—like him. Every nerve-ending came alive and hummed with excitement and need.

She clawed at his shoulders, desperate to touch him, to have him. Moans of sheer pleasure escaped her as he slowly eased out then in again, his rhythm steady, controlled. Electricity zinged through her whole body that seemed to be coming alive for the very first time. Her nipples pebbled painfully and her skin seemed to be on fire. Her mind had turned to mush and she was flailing her head uncontrollably from side to side, all the time mindful of his eyes never leaving her.

Shrouded in his warmth, his safety, she took everything he bestowed upon her—every bite of pain, every drop of pleasure, showering her in him, his care, his soul. As wave after wave of pure ecstasy pounded her body, she lost herself in sheer sensation.

Rising higher and higher on a plane of euphoria, she reached the point of no return and screamed out his name as everything became too much. Tears streamed down her face and sweat poured from her body. His roar filled the air and she felt like she was about to be ripped apart as his hot seed flooded the tiny sack inside her. Blinding realization hit her like a thunderbolt. He had given her his body, now all she craved was his love.

* * * *

83

Kean awoke with an angel in his arms. She was so beautiful, so responsive, so perfect. So why was she here? What the fuck was she doing with *him*?

Bile rose in his throat and he slipped his arm from around her shoulder. She stirred, smiled and rolled her head away from him.

"Shh."

He crept out from under her and headed for the bathroom. Under the heat of the shower, he closed his eyes, trying to slow his mind as it whirled out of control, his thoughts crashing into each other, jumbled and confused.

He turned his face up into the oncoming stream, breathing deeply, his fists clenched. He had slept with her, for fuck's sake. He had just slept with Isla Gillingham. How in the world had that happened? She was a successful model and he was nothing. Every fiber in him wanted this to mean something. The feelings, the passion, the desperation to have her had grown into this enormous 'thing' — one he didn't recognize, didn't understand. Somehow he had felt as though he was giving her himself, his life. The look in her eyes told him she understood that. She wanted it, too. Wanted him. Not only for sex, but for keeps. It didn't make sense so soon, if ever. How could it? Why *would* it?

He took a bottle of gel and smothered it liberally over his skin, trying to rid himself of these feelings — to wash them off him, wash her from his flesh. He scrubbed hard, as though cleansing her from his body would also cleanse her from his mind. She had no purpose there. He knew that. That was the trouble.

Knowing he wouldn't get back to sleep, he dried off, wrapped a towel around him and went to the kitchen. His clothes from yesterday were now dry on a wooden rack in front of the warm oven. Going commando, he pulled on the jeans and one of the sweaters before boiling the kettle for a cup of tea.

Warming the pot, he stared out of the window. The snow had continued to fall all night and was halfway up the door of the outbuilding that sheltered the horses. Although it was only a few minutes after six, it seemed quite bright outside. He knew there was no way this was going to thaw for at least a day or two. As he had predicted, the chances of Isla getting home today were zilch.

The possibility gave him a fuzzy feeling in his stomach. It would be easier all around if that fancy company of hers was to send out a car and take her home — home to the life she was used to, not slumming it out her in the middle of nowhere with a loser like him. But he didn't want her to go. The thought wrenched something inside him that he refused to believe was his heart. Whatever it was, physically ached at the idea of her leaving.

"Penny for them?"

He shot around as her soft voice invaded his contemplation. "What?"

She smiled. "Your thoughts. A penny for your thoughts." She was wrapped in a blanket and her blonde curls bounced haphazardly as she casually shook her head at him.

Kean drank in her beauty. She looked relaxed, happy, gorgeous. The twinkle in her eyes danced merrily as she gazed up at him and her smile broadened. Something in his stomach lurched and he had to quickly close his mouth to prevent a wondrous gasp escaping.

It was unbelievable that he had actually made love to such a gorgeous creature. Even more inconceivable that she was still here, naked under his grandmother's candlewick blanket. And she was smiling.

So why the hell aren't I?

Chapter Ten

Isla narrowed her eyes as she watched Kean scurry out of the back door and over to the shed to see to the horses. Her hands were wrapped around a large mug of tea—apparently Kean didn't usually 'do' coffee—and she shivered under the blanket at the sight of all that snow. It had certainly come down heavy last night and she was grateful to be holed up in the cozy, little cottage.

Kean's demeanor had surprised her and she racked her brains to work out what the problem was. Everything had been absolutely wonderful last night. She had hoped it was the start of something special. He was incredibly gorgeous and such a generous lover. There was more to him than that, though—much more. This guy was a manual laborer and gave the impression of having a few rough edges that just served to make him seem more masculine.

She went to take a shower, remembering how rough he had been with her last night. She had been stunned when he had gone out in the snow to fetch her back and the thrill that had run though her when he had hoisted her over his shoulder like a sack of feathers was one she'd never forget. The indignant rage she'd experienced had suddenly disappeared, sucked into the fire of his eyes as he had stared hungrily at her. She could still hear the panting of their breath and the pounding of their hearts as they stood in his doorway, stalemated. Isla had never seen anyone so beautiful or felt anything so ecstatic.

Taking his gel, she washed his scent onto her body, remembering his hands on her skin the previous night. Their initial fervor had eventually given way to a gentler lovemaking, and she had seen a side to Kean that she'd never imagined was there. He was the most tender, loving man she had ever met, and when he looked at her, it seemed as though he was peering into her very soul, a soul he recognized as kindred.

She quickly dried herself then pulled on the lounge pants he had lent her last night in favor of her jeans, which now sat in a damp heap on the bedroom floor. She looked around. Poor Kean had been so embarrassed at the state of his room, including his own laundry which, she noticed, had miraculously disappeared. He was a lot more sensitive than she'd first thought, and she was glad of it. It didn't explain his manner this morning, though.

He hadn't been rude to her but there was a feeling of discomfort that emanated from him. She had been disappointed, half hoping for a repeat of last night when she caught up with him in the warm kitchen, but the slump of his shoulders had quashed that idea before he had even turned around, staring at her with those hesitant eyes.

Pulling a comb through her wet curls, she was again thankful that she had opted for a shorter style. The thought took her back to Tabitha and her overpowering manner.

Jutting out her chin in the mirror, Isla stood a little straighter. She had tried to stand up for herself where her manager was concerned but still felt downtrodden by her. There was an underlying sense of guilt that prevented her from saying too much to the older woman. She sighed. The feeling was just like the one she had now with Kean. Something wasn't right, but she didn't want to rock the boat by asking him about it. She was a guest in his house, after all.

She gathered up her clothes then headed for the kitchen. Kean had returned, his face red with cold.

"I thought I'd wash these," she said, holding up the laundry.

He looked surprised. "The washing machine's through there." He pointed to a door and she went to investigate.

What she had assumed was a pantry or storage cupboard turned out to be a tiny utility room.

"I was going to put mine in anyway. Leave them on the top there and I'll do them all together." He poured them each another cup of tea.

"Thank you." She did as he'd said then took the drink from him, eyeing him warily. "What are your plans for today — apart from the laundry, I mean?"

He chewed his lip thoughtfully and she wondered for a second whether he was about to address the elephant in the room. He didn't.

"The roads are impassable," he told her decisively.

She nodded — not that she wanted to leave anyhow. "I'll let Tabitha know I won't be back for another day or two." She took a sip of her drink and sat at the small wooden table. "I'd better let Mary-Lou at the magazine know what's happened, too." Isla pulled out her cell and searched for the contact. She had only spoken to the woman a few times but felt like they were life-long friends already.

"Hey, Mary-Lou, it's Isla Gillingham."

She felt right away from Mary-Lou's anxious tone that something was wrong.

"Tabitha Merchant called me earlier," the lady explained. "She said there had been a terrible accident up on the mountain. Your colleague is still at the hospital I hear. Is he all right? Are *you* all right? Where are you? Tabitha was very vague about it all."

"It's okay, Mary-Lou. You honestly don't need to worry," Isla assured her. "Stefan will be home in a day or two and I'm fine, as well. I'm staying with one of the hands from the Fielding Ranch. He has a small cottage at the foot of the mountain, so we came back here after Stefan was rescued. I've got the camera with all the shots from the shoot, but they haven't been edited or anything yet. How soon do you need them?"

She could hear the relief in Mary-Lou's voice. "Well, I could really use them as soon as possible, but I know you won't get through the snow. We're in Almondine, so it's not far from Pelican's Heath, but the roads are totally blocked right now."

At that moment, a beep on Isla's cell informed her that she had a call trying to connect.

"Mary-Lou, can I call you back in a minute? Stefan's trying to get through to me now."

"Of course, dear."

Stefan sounded much perkier than Isla expected. He said he was getting bored and that they were keeping him in for another couple of days to make sure he was all right, but mostly because there was no way he could get transport through in this snow.

"Tabitha's not happy with either of us," Stefan went on with a groan. "Anyone would think we'd done this on purpose."

Isla felt a lurch in her stomach, remembering the accusation that Kean had lobbed at her last night.

"I've just been speaking to Mary-Lou Trotter," she said, swiftly changing the subject. "She was hoping for the photos as soon as possible, but she realizes we can't get them over to her in this weather." She glanced at the window and sighed at the sight of the snow still falling silently over the fields.

"You've got them?" Stefan was clearly astounded. "I thought I took the camera off the ledge with me when I fell."

"No, you dropped it. Kean picked it up. I've got it here."

"There's a little compartment on the side of it," Stefan said excitedly. "In there, you'll find a cable. If you attach that to your iPhone, you can send the pictures to me. I can edit them and send them to the magazine once they're done."

Isla felt a wave of relief wash over her. "Great. I'll get on it now," she promised. "I'll text you Mary-Lou's details, too. How soon do you think you can have them ready?"

"There won't be much work needed on them. I'm a great photographer, you know." Stefan sounded very sure of himself, and Isla rolled her eyes. "I'll probably get them to her by the end of today."

"That's great. I'll tell her to expect them." She chewed her lip thoughtfully for a few seconds. "I'd better call Tabitha, too."

"Good luck with that," Stefan replied. "She was in a foul mood when I spoke to her."

Isla sighed. That was normal for Tabitha. Working for her was never easy.

"Is everythin' all right?" Kean placed a fresh cup of tea in front of her as she ended the call.

She nodded. "Yeah. I just need Stefan's camera. I have to send the pictures to him."

Kean raised his eyebrows. "He wants to work from his hospital bed? Poor bloke *must* be bored."

She nodded, retrieving the camera case from the little hallway.

"He is." She had returned to the kitchen and pulled out the camera.

Finding the little compartment Stefan had indicated, she took out the cable. She'd seen him transfer work from his camera onto his phone and iPad before, so she already had a rough idea what to do.

"I have to ring Tabitha soon, too," she said ruefully as she linked up the devices and began transferring everything across. "It seems *she* thinks the whole thing wasn't an accident, either." She looked accusingly at Kean as he took the seat opposite her, cradling his mug.

He pouted but didn't look up at her.

Isla felt indignant. She had tried to forget about the row they'd had last night that had resulted in her storming out, as the end result had been so wonderful. Seeing Kean's reaction to her this morning, though, had made her wonder whether he was having second thoughts about her, and that could well be the reason. He didn't trust her.

"How long do you expect the snow will last?" she asked cagily.

He shrugged, narrowing his eyes as he looked over at her. "It's forecast for the rest of today, at least. Why? Are you plannin' on going somewhere?"

The ice behind his words was colder than the air outside. She stared at him.

"I wouldn't want to outstay my welcome."

He nodded slowly. "And why would you think you were doin' that?"

She huffed, willing the camera to hurry up and transfer the files. Her stomach roiled as she contemplated her next move. She couldn't endure this atmosphere for another twenty-four hours.

"Because of your attitude toward me today." Her lips tightened and she held her breath, awaiting his response.

He raised one eyebrow.

God, that is sexy.

"Me attitude?"

She nodded. "After making love to me last night, I had expected you to be a little friendlier toward me. Or is that your style? A quick fuck and that's the end of it?"

She trembled and quickly looked down at her hands, holding tightly on to her cell.

He said nothing for a minute, although it felt more like an hour.

"I'm sorry if I've given you that impression," he finally offered.

"What else am I supposed to think?" She noticed that the file had eventually transferred and quickly sent the photos, along with a text to Stefan with Mary-Lou's details. She was glad of something to occupy her fingers while she took a few deep breaths.

He sighed. "We made love last night and it was wonderful," he said quietly.

Her breathing hitched. His tone had changed completely and she looked up at him, surprised to see how sad he appeared.

"I don't know what you want me to do," he admitted

with a shrug. "We didn't talk about it at the time and it just seemed crass to discuss it this morning."

"Did it mean anything to you?" She held her breath, envisaging grabbing her coat and disappearing into the snow again. Would he come after her a second time? Would she want him to? She shuddered.

Kean's warm, brown eyes surprised her. He seemed much more sensitive now, somehow. More like he had been last night.

He huffed. "I'm not in the habit of takin' young women to my bed," he announced. "Of course it meant somethin'."

She gaped at him. Not that she would expect him to admit it even if he *was* in the habit of bedding young women, but with his looks and that sexy Irish accent, he could easily have any girl he wanted. To hear that last night had actually meant something to him gave her an unexpected thrill as butterflies danced in her stomach.

"It meant something to me, too." Her voice wasn't much above a whisper.

He raised both eyebrows in surprise. "Really?"

Her blood suddenly rose to boiling point and she stared at him, horrified. "You don't believe me?"

"I didn't say that."

"You implied it."

"Did I?"

"Yes, you damn well did. And I know you didn't believe that Stefan falling off a cliff was an accident. You seriously don't trust me, do you, Kean? I'm surprised you've let me in your house at all. Aren't you afraid I'm going to steal something?"

She quickly gathered up the camera and stuffed it back into its bag.

"I haven't called you a thief."

She was stunned at his response and stared up at him, suddenly halting her actions. "What?"

"Just because I questioned whether you had planned Stefan's accident doesn't mean I've accused you of stealing."

He sounded quite matter of fact.

"So you *do* think I planned it?" She spat the words at him.

"I don't know. You certainly had the motive, and I knew from the start there was always a chance that you'd try something like that."

She felt her face glow with anger. "Oh yeah? And just how did you know that, Sherlock?"

His passive manner infuriated her even more as he took a deep breath.

"Come off it. You're a successful, wealthy model. Everyone around you gets to make money off you in some way or another. Your legal team's watchin' your every move for an opportunity to swoop in and sue whoever they can to put a bit more into the pot. You were up a mountain in the snow. I would have been a fool not to expect you to try something." He gave a self-deprecating snigger.

"How fucking *dare* you?" she screamed at him.

To her horror, he rolled his eyes. "Here we go again. Shall I get your coat for you?"

Isla felt like she was about to be sick and wasn't sure if it was anger or disappointment that was worse.

She shook her head, mortified. Her brain whirled as she tried to decipher what he was saying. None of it made any sense.

"Why do you think like that?" she demanded. "You don't even *know* me."

He pursed his lips. "No, but I know *of* you."

"What you've read in the magazines?" She racked her brain to remember whether there had ever been anything derogatory or scandalous written about her. She wasn't a celebrity by any means, so she was lucky in that respect. She didn't have to worry about paparazzi waiting on every corner or reporters trying to dig up the dirt on her. Some of the other girls she had worked with had contended with some awful incidents, but not her.

He shook his head. "Don't flatter yourself, darlin'. I haven't read any of the material you'd appear in. I only go on what I've heard."

"From your buddies? People who don't know the first thing about me but are happy to make stuff up for their own amusement?" She stood over him, her hands on her hips.

He looked a little taken aback. "No. The Fieldings told us a little about your success when they briefed us about you usin' some of their land for your photo shoot. Then I was told certain things by your manager."

His dismissive attitude was getting on her last nerve, but his words cut like a knife.

"What *certain things*?"

He sighed again. "Well, she told me you were quite a commodity and I needed to keep you safe. And she told me about your powerful lawyers who would sue my ass for every penny if anythin' happened to you."

"And you took that to mean that I was going to stage some sort of incident so that I could file a claim against you?" Her voice had raised a few pitches as indignation flooded her bones.

Kean gave her a dry look. "I know you think I'm just a cowboy with no brains, but I can read between the lines, you know. I can recognize a subliminal threat when I hear one, believe you me."

"Subliminal threat?" She snarled at him.

He tightened his lips. "I was there. I know what that woman was tellin' me."

She was surprised at how firm he was about his assertions. She took a step backward for a minute, trying to gather her thoughts. Tabitha could be a real bitch at times and she could certainly imagine her threatening to sue Kean if anything had gone wrong up the mountain. She had a way of telling you something without actually spelling it out, and Kean seemed intuitive enough to pick up the vibes. Perhaps he had read her manager right.

A heavy thud hit the pit of her stomach at the realization and she slowly sat back down.

"So, Tabitha threatened you, and when something actually happened, you chose to believe that it was because of what she'd said instead of assessing the situation that you had actually witnessed?" It made sense. Tabitha's powers of persuasion knew no limits, and once she'd planted that seed in the guy's head, he couldn't be blamed for misreading the signs.

He ran a hand though his hair, sitting forward with his elbows on the table between them. "I didn't know what to think," he admitted. "From what I saw, it looked like a complete accident. You cried out and he jumped and fell backward. It was —"

"Just that you chose to believe Tabitha," she finished for him.

Kean fidgeted uncomfortably. "I didn't *choose* anythin'. I couldn't be sure, that's all. Not at the time."

She stared at him. "And now?"

He shook his head slowly. "Now I know she was one prize bitch who was out to make trouble." He shrugged. "It was an accident. If she hadn't said all that beforehand, I wouldn't have even considered anythin' else. I was stupid enough to let her words get to me. I'm sorry."

His voice was soft and his face looked sunken.

"So, what changed your mind?"

"You."

She swallowed hard, suddenly feeling her whole body relax. Unable to hold his gaze, she busied herself studying her fingers that fiddled with an imaginary piece of cotton on the tablecloth.

"I should never have doubted you. I should have trusted you all along." His words were music to her ears but there was a sadness behind them that concerned her.

"But?" She glanced up at him, almost afraid to hear what he had to say next.

He sighed and leaned back in his chair. "I'm sorry. I was wrong about you being untrustworthy, but it doesn't alter the fact that you are who you are and things shouldn't have gotten out of hand last night."

"What?" She frowned, tensing right back up.

He closed his eyes momentarily then looked back at her, his pupils big and dark. "I shouldn't have made love to you last night. You're right. I don't know you. For all I know, you could be married or have a boyfriend. I shouldn't have assumed you were available."

"I am 'available'." She used air quotes. "Don't you think I would have stopped you if I had been in a relationship with someone else? Do you think I merely sleep with anyone who makes a move on me?" She was starting to get annoyed again now as hurt swept through her.

He shook his head. "No."

"So we've ascertained that your assumption I was free was correct. Why is there a problem then?"

"I just feel that it shouldn't have happened. You don't know me, Isla. If you did, you wouldn't be here. Believe me." His big brown eyes pleaded with her to understand, but she didn't. How could she?

"In that case, I think you'd better tell me."

Chapter Eleven

Kean felt a huge lump settle in his gut. This wasn't what he was hoping for. Far from it. She should have been so indignant that he had mistrusted her in the first place that she maintained the anger he had seen pouring from her only a few moments ago. That would have been so much easier.

"I have to go see to the horses," he claimed, standing up.

"Great. I'll help."

He was stunned to see her go through to the hallway and pull on her boots and coat. She wasn't going to give up. *Damn!*

"I can manage. I only have to check on them and make sure they've got enough water. Why don't you stay here in the warmth?"

His suggestion fell on deaf ears.

"Come on. We'll get it done in half the time with two of us then we can *both* get back where it's warm."

Reluctantly, he shrugged on his coat and followed her out the back door. It was late morning and the snow still continued to fall. The sky looked heavy and the silence of the landscape was almost suffocating.

They topped off the water and feed for the horses, and Kean was glad to note there was plenty of hay to keep them warm for another couple of days at least.

"Is that everything?" Isla was patting the nose of the horse she had ridden yesterday.

Kean momentarily hid his head in the flank of one of the others, his mind racing.

"Kean, are you all right?" Her voice was full of concern,

which made him feel guilty.

He raised his head. "Yes. Come on. Let's get inside."

After fastening the door to the shed, he turned slowly to follow her back inside. She sure was beautiful. Her blonde curls danced in the dim sunlight and her slender body strolled gracefully through the snow. Every bit of her was feminine and elegant. She was almost at the back door when she turned toward him. Her face glowed with the cold but she didn't look tense at all. She smiled back at him.

"Come on, slowpoke," she called over, teasingly.

He couldn't help but grin back at her sass. Shaking his head, he stomped back through the snow until he caught up with her on his now-hidden doorstep.

"What kept you?" She was certainly in a fun mood as they went into the warm kitchen and removed their coats and boots.

"Some of us had work to do," he told her in a mock-stern voice. "The shed door had to be secured, you know. We need to keep the horses as warm as we can and make sure they're safe." He put the kettle on to boil.

She nodded, pursing her lips as though concentrating on his every word. "Oh, right. It's a good job you're here, cowboy. I wouldn't have had a clue about any of that."

"Are you mockin' me?" he asked, feigning horror.

She looked thoughtful for a second. "Yes," she admitted with a giggle.

"Well, I think that's a wee bit cheeky, young lady."

He put his hands on his hips.

She was still smiling but looked a little unsure of his reaction. "So what are you going to do about it?" She stuck her nose in the air playfully, her hazel eyes twinkling with mirth.

"Wouldn't you just like to know?" He warmed the teapot. Once he'd placed it back on the counter, he tapped his temple. "It's all gettin' stored up here. Don't you worry," he assured her, making her giggle even more.

She was still smiling as she plunked herself down on the

chair she had used earlier. Her cell was on the table in front of her and he noticed her expression completely change as she caught sight of it.

"Is everything okay?" He knew it wasn't.

"Tabitha rang." Her voice was quiet, hesitant. "She wants me to call her right back."

He frowned, placing the two cups of tea on the table. "I can go and —"

"No, no it's fine. It won't be private. Do you mind if I do it now?"

He shrugged. "The sooner the better, I'd say. Get it over with." She was obviously dreading making the call but knew it had to be done.

Her fingers trembled as she pressed a few keys on her cell and she took a long breath while she waited for the answer.

"Hi, Tabitha. It's me, Isla." She was clearly trying her best to sound cheerful, though her face told a totally different story.

Although Kean couldn't hear what was being said on the other end, he could make out the smarmy tone.

"I'm sorry. I did mean to call you," Isla explained. "I spoke to Stefan and sent the photos over to him. He's editing them and sending them on to Mary-Lou at the magazine."

Isla was obviously hoping her manager would be pleased with her progress, but the lady certainly didn't seem that way, if her raised voice was anything to go by.

"How dare I undermine you?" Isla said incredulously.

Kean was taken aback by Tabitha's manner. He eyed Isla warily. She seemed to shrink back in her chair.

"I was only trying to help," she said. "Mary-Lou wanted the photos as quickly as possible. I had them here, so it made sense to send them over to Stefan to finish off."

·Kean couldn't hear what was said next, but Isla shook her head.

"It wasn't like that, Tabitha. No one's cutting you out of any loop. Stefan's going to be there for another couple of days and he said he was bored. He was glad of something useful to do. Besides, we have to keep the client happy, don't we?"

Her efforts to appease the woman clearly failed miserably and Isla's shoulders slumped in defeat.

"I'm sorry, Tabitha. It wasn't meant like that. I was simply trying to do the right thing, that's all. I'm stranded here and Stefan's stuck over at the hospital in town. We couldn't just do nothing now, could we?"

Tabitha's rant was audible, although her actual words weren't — not that Kean wanted to listen to her anyway. He was concerned at how deflated Isla had become since the call and clenched his fists to stop himself from grabbing the phone out of her hand. He would love to tell Tabitha Merchant exactly what he thought of her. She was a manipulative trouble-maker and a bully. Unfortunately, they were traits that were all too familiar to him and his stomach churned at the idea of having to explain that to Isla.

She was still apologizing as she put down her cell, and her eyes looked heavy with unshed tears.

"You shouldn't let her speak to you like that," he said gently.

"I don't have much choice."

"Why?"

She wiped the back of her hand over eyes before lifting her mug. "I sort of owe her."

Kean balked in surprise. "Oh." He was desperate to ask her why but was well aware it was none of his business. And besides, he wouldn't like it if she probed into his affairs.

She took a long sip of her tea, leaning forward in her chair again and casually placing her elbows on the table.

"Tabitha sort of came to my rescue when I needed some help," she told him. "The magazine I'd been working with folded and my work quickly dried up. I honestly thought I was going to have to give up fashion and modeling altogether."

"Fashion?" She had taken him by surprise.

"I used to do more than just modeling," she told him, nodding. "I was already studying fashion when I was offered work as a model. I didn't want to give up my education, so Beryl Boothroyd let me do both for a while. I worked with the fashion editor, getting collections together and finding the right models to display them. They sent me on some great training courses and I learned everything I needed to know while I was still working on the editing side. I loved doing both. When the magazine folded, though, I thought my world had ended. Then Tabitha came along and offered to manage me."

"As a model?"

"Yes. She said there was more money in it, and at the time, I desperately needed it to help my sister who was in a psychiatric hospital. I paid for all her treatment. I managed to get her the best. She's fine now and married to a wonderful man. You honestly wouldn't know there had ever been anything wrong with her." She smiled in a way that showed her pride in what she'd done.

"That's good." Kean nodded.

"Anyhow, Tabitha had seen some of my modeling work and told me to stick with it. I was a little disappointed, to be honest, as I loved working in fashion, but needs must and I was grateful for the chance of some work."

She looked a little sad.

"I was truly grateful that she took me on her books, and she eventually got me some good jobs."

"But you still miss the fashion side?" He could see the answer in her eyes, although she seemed a little embarrassed to admit it.

She nodded slowly. "It's not that I'm ungrateful or anything," she added quickly.

"Gratitude doesn't always equal happiness," he told her with a pout.

"But I *am* happy."

He was surprised at how defensive she seemed, all of a

sudden. He raised his eyebrows, studying her carefully. "Are you?"

She looked stunned. "Of course."

"You didn't look all that happy when you were on the phone." He noticed her face fall and she quickly looked away, turning slightly red.

"It's just…"

"What?"

She huffed uncomfortably. "Sometimes she makes me feel…sort of…stupid."

Kean felt his mouth gape open and he quickly shut it. "Stupid?"

She nodded, her curls bouncing beautifully around her flushed face.

"Why would she do that?"

Isla shrugged. "I don't know. I thought I was doing the right thing getting the photos edited and sent over to Mary-Lou Trotter. She said she needed them as soon as possible, only…"

He was surprised at her lack of confidence. "Only Tabitha wasn't happy that you'd used your initiative?"

She looked up at him through her long lashes. "She believed I was undermining her. Usually Stefan would edit the pictures and pass them on to Tabitha. She would check them over before letting the client have them. I shouldn't have tried to take over like that."

Kean felt his stomach lurch at how small she suddenly appeared. She was a little more slumped in her chair now and her voice was quiet. She was also blushing profusely. Pity mixed with anger inside him and he chewed his lip thoughtfully to prevent himself from saying the wrong thing in haste.

"But surely the most important thing is to keep the client happy?" he managed after a minute or so.

"That's what I thought."

"But Tabitha believed her pride was more important?"

Isla's eyes widened.

"Why would she need to check the photographs? Surely Stefan's the photographer and the best judge of whether or not the pictures work?" His voice was a little tighter than he had intended as he imagined Tabitha Merchant running roughshod over everyone.

"Well...I suppose," she murmured.

"So, she's a control freak?"

Isla gaped at him as though the idea had never occurred to her. "Well...um." She looked unnerved.

"It's okay. You don't have to say anythin'. I could tell when I first saw her."

Isla sighed. "She's not all bad."

"Really? She practically lied to me about you. She wanted me to think you were some kind of spoiled diva who would stop at nothin' to make a few bucks out of me, even if it meant closin' down the Fielding Ranch. I'd call that pretty bad." His blood boiled as he spoke and tried his best to keep the anger from his voice.

Isla squirmed, still nursing her now-empty teacup.

"I'm sorry," he went on, his voice a little gentler. "I shouldn't have listened to her. I'm usually not a bad judge of character and it seems that even though I'd got her measure right away, I shouldn't have let her sway me. It wasn't fair on you." He felt his shoulders slump a little.

Isla looked up at him in surprise. "You've nothing to apologize for," she assured him. "Tabitha has a way of convincing you of things even when you know she's talking trash. It's just a knack she seems to have."

He smiled, grateful for her understanding. "But she tried to put a rift between us and I almost let her," he admitted, ruefully. "I should have stuck to me own instincts."

She swallowed hard, looking a little embarrassed as she quickly averted her eyes to her cup.

"Look. I know she's your boss, but I honestly don't think she's the sort of person you need to be working for, if you don't mind me sayin'." He wondered if she would be annoyed with him for speaking his mind, but she simply looked up at him in surprise. "There must be other jobs you could take." He shrugged.

"I suppose so," she admitted. "I've often thought how nice it would be to leave Merchant's and go to work for someone who actually valued me. I'd love to get back into fashion, too." She looked a little wistful and he felt a pang in his chest.

"Well, you're livin' in a big city. I'm sure there must be other jobs out there," he said, standing up and taking the cups to the sink.

He was surprised when she didn't reply and turned back around to face her after placing the crockery on the counter.

"I don't know that I'd want to continue living in the city if I didn't have to," she told him quietly.

Kean's heart lurched as he realized how unhappy she must be. "I thought you were settled with your friend." He narrowed his eyes, leaning back against the sink to study her further. She looked totally miserable and he wondered if it was his fault for bringing up the subject.

She looked over at him, her eyes big and watery. "I was."

He watched as she slowly stood up and went to look out the window. The snow had stopped falling at last.

"I think I'll go check on the horses again," she told him, clearly fighting back tears.

He wanted to go over and put an arm around her, but he wasn't sure it would be the right move. She looked as though she was desperate for a little time on her own to think.

"I'll get these dishes done then I'll follow you out," he offered. He didn't mind allowing her a little time to herself but he was darned if he was going to leave her for too long.

He turned back to the sink and ran the hot water as she got ready and went out the back. From his position, he watched her stroll through the thick snow to the shed. She wiped her hand over her face a couple of times and he guessed she was crying. It took all his resolve not to run out after her.

He quickly washed the cups and left them to drain, before

preparing some lunch. Then he pulled on his boots and coat and set off to find Isla. He caught up with her in the shed. She obviously hadn't heard his arrival as she was chatting away to the horses.

"You are incredibly beautiful," she was telling them, "and so well-behaved. Whoever trained you certainly knew what he was doing. I've never known such obedient horses." She patted the flank of one while snuggling up to another.

Kean stood in the entrance where the door had been left slightly ajar. She obviously hadn't noticed him.

"I'm not leaving you out either, boy," she continued, going over to the third horse and stroking its nose. "You're all so gorgeous. I'll miss you when I leave here." She sighed.

Kean's stomach roiled with sickness. He would certainly miss her when she left, too. Her whole body seemed much more relaxed as she fussed the large beasts, checking their feed and water while lavishing all her attention on them. She looked quite at home here with the animals, which surprised him, seeing as she was a city girl, but then, hadn't she said she was originally from the country?

Her eyes shone and her face glowed as she chatted away to the horses, and he felt a little guilty for intruding. Would she think he was spying on her?

The big smile that broadened as she saw him watching her told him that she hadn't taken offense.

"I didn't see you there," she admitted.

"I know."

She frowned slightly. "Have you been there long?"

He shook his head. "No."

She seemed a little relieved. "I think they've got everything they need."

"What about you?" He cocked his head sideways.

She stopped patting the horse and looked at him a little quizzically. "What do you mean?"

"You look quite at home in here with them." He nodded toward the horses.

She smiled, looking a little relieved. "Who wouldn't be?

They're lovely." She patted the one in front of her once more before turning to walk toward him.

He nodded. "Come on. I've put some soup on to warm," he said.

Her eyes lit up even more. "Ooh, lovely."

She waited while he secured the shed and they began the trek back toward the house.

"Oops!" She nearly slid when they neared the hidden step and she reached out for his arm.

He instinctively caught her and pulled her toward him to stop her falling. "Careful."

The world seemed to stop spinning for a moment as he held her, her beautiful rosy face turned up to him. Her mouth was slightly open and her eyes were wide. She was the most beautiful woman he had ever seen.

"Thank you," she whispered.

He couldn't reply. His throat was dry and his mouth was rigid. He had no idea what he must have looked like as he gawked down at her like some gormless oaf.

Despite the snow, her body felt warm next to his and his mind was automatically whisked back to last night when he had held her naked body in his arms. He cursed himself for being so moody this morning. He had ruined everything with his thoughts of unworthiness. He was stupid. So what if he didn't deserve a girl like her? Surely that was her choice as much as his? He had a duty to explain everything to her. At least she could make an informed decision if she knew all the facts.

He smiled at her gorgeous face. "Come on. The soup'll be ready."

After he ushered her inside, they stamped the snow from their boots on the doormat before removing them and their coats and placing them on the rack in front of the stove. They would dry much quicker there than out in the tiny hallway.

"It's so lovely and cozy in here," she said, looking around with a smile.

Kean warmed at her approval. His earlier fears that she was used to much better than this had dissipated as he realized that she was just as down to earth as he had first hoped.

He took some warm bread from the oven and placed it on a tray with two bowls of hot soup.

Isla beamed as he put the tray on the table in front of her.

"It smells divine," she enthused, taking one of the bowls.

"Let's hope it tastes as good." He sat opposite her and tucked into his lunch. It was delicious and he was pleased to hear Isla's moans of delight as she ate hers.

"I could get used to this," she said with a grin, as she broke more bread from her roll.

Kean's breath hitched. He would love to think of her spending more time here with him, but was it likely?

"Wouldn't you miss the bright lights of the city?" he asked, holding his breath for her response.

She smiled, shaking her head. "Not a bit. I much prefer it out here," she said. "I only live there because it's where the work is."

Kean felt a grain of hope well inside him. "Are you serious? What about your friend?"

She sighed and he wondered if he hadn't just spoiled the moment as her face fell.

"It was very good of Verity to invite me to stay with them, but I'm much happier out of there," she explained, a little sadly. "Her new boyfriend's— Well…he gives me the creeps, to be honest." She bit her lip.

Kean guessed there was more to this than met the eye. "Has he done anythin' to make you feel that way?"

She blushed and he knew he'd hit the nail right on the head.

"He made a pass at me. More than once." She sounded hesitant.

"Did you tell him where to go?"

He was surprised when she stared up at him then giggled. "I love your turn of phrase," she told him.

Kean grinned. "Well, I'm glad I amuse you," he said. "So, what happened?" He finished the last of his bread roll and rubbed the crumbs from his fingers.

Isla huffed. "The first time, he tried to kiss me. I pushed him off and told him I wasn't interested, but I tried to keep it lighthearted, you know? The next time, he grabbed my shoulders and forced his lips against mine. I had to dig my nails into his face to get him off me. He was real mad." She took a deep breath.

"I take it there were no witnesses?" Kean felt bile rise in his throat.

She shook her head. "He also used to make lewd comments about knowing how much I wanted him and saying how nice I'd look without my clothes on. It wasn't just what he said but also the way he said it—sort of menacing, threatening almost."

Kean stared at her. "Did he touch you?"

"No. He said he couldn't wait to get me into bed, though. I didn't know what to do. He got braver as time went on, whispering to me when Verity was only in the next room. It was almost as if he was daring me to make a fuss."

"You didn't tell her, then?"

She bit her lip. "I couldn't. I knew she'd be hurt and I didn't want that."

"So you put up with it?" He tried to keep the annoyance from his voice.

"Sort of. I started taking more and more jobs on location."

"Basically, he scared you out of your home?"

"No. Well…not quite. It was her place, not mine. I started looking for somewhere new so I could leave them to it, but I was away that often I didn't get around to viewing anywhere. Besides, I was afraid that Verity would be offended if I moved out."

"You didn't talk to her about it, then?"

"No. How could I? Her last boyfriend cheated on her. I could hardly tell her that this one wanted to do the same thing—but with *me*."

Kean said nothing. He knew only too well how it felt to be trapped because of being indebted to someone. The world was a cruel place to live in, sometimes.

Chapter Twelve

After lunch Kean had some paperwork to do for the ranch so Isla took the opportunity to call Mary-Lou to see if the photos had arrived yet.

"They're wonderful," the other lady enthused, seemingly glad to hear from her. "And thank you so much for getting them to me as quickly as you did. I usually have to wait days to get anything through after a shoot, and I was afraid that on this occasion we would miss the deadline."

"Stefan did all the editing," Isla told her. "I'm glad you like them."

"Like them? I *love* them, dear! In fact, I'd like you to do more work for me—paid next time, of course. Having advertised that you would be in the new issue has already amassed a load of pre-orders. We'll have to double our normal print numbers."

"Well, that's good to hear." Isla felt a warmth flood through her veins, knowing that she had helped in some way. "And, of course, I'd love to do more work for you. I absolutely adore it out here, Mary-Lou. It reminds me of my childhood."

"Wonderful! I'll have to contact a few Cavern County clothing suppliers and see if they would be willing to buy space in the magazine. I'm keen to promote the local businesses, you see."

"I think that's a great idea. You tell me what you need and when, and I'm sure I'll be able to fit it in. I'll just need to let Tabitha know." The thought filled her with dread. Speaking to Tabitha about anything was never easy, but when it came to having her own ideas about her future, Isla felt like she was walking on eggshells.

"I'm going to call her this afternoon, anyhow," Mary-Lou told her. "I want to congratulate her on her staff. For Stefan to do all this work from his hospital bed and for you to organize it from wherever it is you're holed up is fabulous. I've never worked with such resourceful people before."

Isla swallowed hard. Most bosses would be glad to hear praise for their staff, especially from a new client who was keen to send more work their way. Tabitha wasn't like most bosses, though.

"Okay, thank you," she managed.

"Some of these pictures truly are remarkable," Mary-Lou went on, clearly flicking through them as she spoke.

"Stefan's a brilliant photographer," Isla agreed. "One of the best I've worked with."

"He's certainly talented," Mary-Lou said. "And you look positively radiant in some of these."

Isla frowned. She was sitting on the sofa in the living room, staring into the dancing flames of the fire Kean had lit for her before going to do his work on the kitchen table.

"Right, well, I'll get on. I'm sure you've got things to do, dear. I'll have a word with Tabitha and hopefully one of us will be able to give you some good news about some future work."

"Thanks, Mary-Lou. I appreciate that."

She clicked off her cell, deep in thought. The shoot had been to promote the clothes that a factory in Almondine had been manufacturing. Their sales had taken a dive of late and they were hoping that some exposure might help raise their profile—and their profits. She had been pleased to help out. When she had worked on the magazine in her early days, she had liaised with many companies who needed a boost to their sales without paying out too much for advertising. It had been one of her favorite parts of the job, made all the better when they saw the results of her efforts.

Kean was talking on his phone when she went through to

the kitchen to make a cup of tea. Although she usually stuck to coffee, she was enjoying the change and made a mental note to drink more tea when she got home. She pointed to the kettle and he nodded eagerly.

"Everythin's fine, boss," he was saying. "Isla's stayin' here and I've got the horses fed and watered. They're in the big shed. I told Aiden all about it last night. He didn't have a problem with it."

Isla boiled the kettle and got the teapot and cups ready, trying not to listen in on the conversation.

Kean huffed, clearly exasperated. "No, everythin's fine."

He held his cell up to her. "Isla, would you kindly let my boss know that I haven't murdered you in your sleep or anythin'?"

She grinned and took the phone. "Hello?"

"Miss Gillingham, it's Ben Fielding here...from the ranch."

"Hi, Mr. Fielding, how are you?" She was surprised at his concerned tone.

"I'm afraid I got stuck in Almondine last night. I just got back here courtesy of a local tractor, of all things. Nothing else can move in this snow."

"Yes, it is thick. We managed to get to Kean's house before it got too bad, fortunately, but I don't think we'll be going anywhere for a while. Is everything all right?"

"I didn't realize he'd taken you back there," Ben explained. "We would gladly put you up here at the ranch. I can get a tractor over to fetch you if you don't mind a rough ride?"

Isla swallowed hard. The last thing she wanted to do was leave Kean, but how could she explain that to his boss?

"Oh no, don't go to any trouble on my account, Mr. Fielding. I'm fine where I am, honestly. Kean's a wonderful host and he's looking after me extremely well. I'm loving it out here." She smiled, hoping he would detect how happy she was and stop worrying.

"Well...if you're sure?" Ben Fielding sounded anything *but* sure.

She laughed. "Of course."

"You're not finding it a little…uncomfortable?"

"No. Why would I?" She frowned now, trying to fathom what his problem was.

"He's not the most sociable of people, Miss Gillingham. Although he's great at his job—the best, in fact—he's not exactly a…a people person, if you know what I mean?"

Bile roiled in her stomach and she felt indignant at his words. Kean placed a cup of tea on the table beside her, his eyes wide and worried.

"I can assure you that I am being very well looked after and am quite happy to stay as long as Kean will have me. As I said, he's the perfect host—great company, thoughtful and helpful. I couldn't ask for better hospitality." She was aware that she sounded a little more curt than she intended, although it seemed to do the job.

"All right, Miss Gillingham, as long as you're sure. I wanted to check that you were comfortable."

"I am, Mr. Fielding. Thank you for your concern."

She handed the cell back to Kean who took it silently from her. His papers were strewn across the table next to his laptop and she guessed he was still working. She heard him speaking to his boss again as she took her tea into the living room. Curling up on the sofa, she recalled just how accommodating her host had been last night. She smiled. His manner had surprised her this morning and she had begun to wonder if he'd regretted making love to her, but the way he'd looked at her when she'd slipped on the snow earlier spoke volumes. He didn't regret anything. Far from it, if the heat behind those eyes was anything to go by.

"Thanks for sayin' that."

She looked up in surprise. "What?"

He sat on the sofa next to her with a heavy sigh. "When you told Ben that I was lookin' after you well. He was worried when Aiden told him where you were…where you'd spent the night."

"Why?" She took a sip of her tea.

Kean ran a hand through his dark hair with a grimace. "It may have escaped your notice, but I'm not the most sociable of people. I think they were afraid we'd sat here in silence for the past twenty-four hours and that I'd starved you half to death."

She giggled, leaning toward him conspiratorially. "Then they don't know either of us very well, do they?"

Kean's face instantly relaxed and he grinned back at her. *God, he looks gorgeous!*

"I think we were anythin' *but* silent last night." His eyes twinkled as he smiled cheekily.

Isla felt a stirring in her pussy and clenched her thighs together tightly.

His giggle made her wonder if he had noticed.

"A gentleman wouldn't mention a thing like that." She pouted playfully, sitting upright again.

He leaned into her, drowning her in his masculine scent. "A gentleman wouldn't fling a woman over his shoulder and take her to bed with him," he murmured.

Isla felt her whole body reach boiling point as she squeezed her thighs together even tighter to try to quell the reaction of her pussy that threatened to flood her borrowed pants. Her jaw slackened as he winked at her, stood then marched back to the kitchen.

* * * *

Kean snickered to himself as he took a bowl of frozen stew from the freezer. There was plenty there for both of them, and it would save him having to abandon his gorgeous house guest any longer than was necessary. He guessed she would need a little time to herself right now, though, and after putting their supper to defrost, he tidied away his papers.

He was glad that Cordell trusted him with some of the ranch's bookkeeping and hoped it was a sign that he was thought of highly enough to be considered for the assistant foreman's job. His logical brain made short work of the figures and Cordell had even commented that Kean was quicker at balancing the books than he was.

Kean looked around the little cottage that wasn't really much more than a shack. He was glad to have the roof over his head and not to have to rely on anyone else for it, but it wasn't good enough for company — especially not the kind of company he had sitting in his living room right now. It had been his ambition since starting work at the Fielding Ranch to get promoted to a decent position — one in which he would be respected, admired even. More to the point, he wanted a position that would earn him enough money to pay his dad back every penny he owed him. He grimaced, knowing that it wasn't only hard cash he owed his old man. Dad had saved his arse on too many occasions to remember.

He took a deep breath. He was going to have to explain all that to Isla, whether he liked it or not. And he knew for a fact that *she* wasn't going to like it.

He went through to the sitting room just as Isla's cell rang.

"Hi, Mary-Lou, how are you?" She sounded delighted to hear from the woman.

Kean stoked the fire, aware of how quickly Isla's mood changed.

"What?"

She looked devastated and he had to stop himself from going over and putting an arm around her shoulder. Something wasn't right.

"But...can she do that? I mean...she doesn't *own* me, does she?" Isla was clearly close to tears. "Leave it with me, Mary-Lou. I'll get back to you. And don't worry, okay?" Her hand trembled as she took the phone from her ear and gazed at it.

Kean slid onto the sofa next to her. "What's happened?"

When she looked up at him, tears fell from her beautiful brown eyes. She shook her head. "Mary-Lou wants me to do more work for the magazine but Tabitha's told her I can't do it." She squeezed her full lips together and sniffed.

"Why?"

Isla shrugged. "She's told Mary-Lou that this was only a one-off and she can't release me for any work. Furthermore, it's not good for my reputation or my career."

Her jaw was tense as she fought back the tears and Kean had to use all his restraint not to hold her.

"Can she do that?" His brain raced.

"She thinks she can."

He frowned. "But surely it's up to you. It's *your* life. You can't just live it for everyone else. What do *you* want to do?"

She looked up at him helplessly. "I love it here," she said. "I'd work out here all the time if I could. I was over the moon when Mary-Lou said she had more work for me. I actually started thinking things were going to work out, you know?"

He nodded. "Yeah, I gathered that."

He'd seen the look on her face when Mary-Lou had asked her. He'd heard her tell Ben Fielding that she would like to stay here as long as he'd have her — as if he'd ever want her to leave.

She took out a cotton handkerchief from the sleeve of her sweater and wiped her face.

"It's not that easy, though, is it? I'm signed to Merchant's. I'm under contract. If I wanted to break the agreement, it would cost me a fortune — a fortune I don't have." She sniffed again. "Besides, I feel —"

"That you owe the evil bitch?" He couldn't believe she still felt like that after the way she was being treated.

She nodded miserably. "I don't know where I'd be without her."

"Wherever it was, I'd bet you'd be much happier there," he replied, fighting back his anger.

"I'm happy here." Her voice was soft and her big eyes were staring into his.

Kean leaned forward as a fire raged in his belly. He tasted salt on her lips as he kissed her and ran a hand through her soft curls.

She stroked his neck as she kissed him back—a kiss that became more fervent with every second that passed.

He couldn't hold her close enough. He wanted to devour her whole body right then and there. Her gasps told him she felt the same as she crashed her lips together with his and ripped her nails through his scalp.

Tugging at each other's clothes, they managed to strip as the fire sent shadows dancing all around them.

"I want you," he breathed into her mouth.

She moaned her assent.

Kean didn't need telling twice. He spun her around so she was standing in front of the sofa and put his arms over hers as he placed her hands on the back of it. Her skin was like satin next to his and he wanted to be touching every part of her body at once.

She turned her head over her left shoulder and smiled at him, her breath panting hard.

"Please, Kean."

He ran his fingers over her sodden pussy then up her tight channel. She was more than ready and he could tell by the way she tensed that she wouldn't be able to hold off much longer.

"Kean!" she urged.

His thick cock nudged her pussy, which almost sucked him into her.

He groaned at the sensation and followed through, relishing her gasp as he forged into her.

"My God, Kean!"

She was close. Real close.

Her enthusiasm drove him on and he plowed repeatedly through her soft folds and into her hot, wet channel.

His release was imminent and he thrust harder.

"I'm coming! Kean, I'm coming!" She screamed her climax, tipping him over the edge and his cock tensed one more time before shooting its seed clean into her body.

Nothing had ever felt so good. Nothing had ever felt the same.

"I love you," he whispered into her ear before slumping onto the sofa while she did the same.

He held her in his arms, not wanting to ever let her go. The late afternoon sun afforded very little light, and the fire was already dying, shooting strange shadows all around them.

Isla panted hard into his chest, her beautiful body rising and falling with each labored breath. His torso was wet, which he assumed was from the sweat that rolled off both their sated bodies. It took a few minutes for him to realize that she was shaking and was horrified to look down and see that she was sobbing quietly.

The dreamy state suddenly vanished from his mind and he was wide awake in an instant. "What is it, darling?"

She shook her head, not wanting to move. "It's okay," she assured him, eventually lifting her face to his. "I'm just so happy. I finally know what love is and it's made me realize that nothing in my past has ever compared to this. I love you, Kean. I really love you."

Her eyes were wide and the firelight caught the tears that gathered there. She was looking up, pleading with him to understand. He did. He felt the same.

Bending down, he took her mouth in a lingering kiss that tingled right down to his groin. Her lips were plump and salty and her tongue thick and soft. He explored the inside of her mouth before gently nibbling her lips then kissing the tears from her cheeks. Something stirred inside him but he knew it wouldn't be appropriate to make love to her again just yet. He held her tightly before whispering in her ear, "I need to use the bathroom."

She giggled. It was a delightful sound and a relief to see her face relax as she smiled up at him.

The air in the hall was like ice as he headed toward the bathroom naked. He shuddered, hurrying as fast as he could. The sweat seemed to freeze to his skin and he made a mental note to get thicker carpets fitted before next winter.

He automatically put his hand down to remove the

condom as his mind wondered whether things would be much different by the time next winter came around. Would Isla still want him? He knew his feelings for her were genuine and was thrilled with what she'd said, despite them only knowing each other for a short while.

His stomach thudded as he suddenly realized that there was nothing covering his throbbing cock. He'd forgotten the condom! Sickness roiled inside him as his mind recounted their earlier escapades. Having become completely engrossed, it hadn't occurred to him to go fetch a condom. In fact, wild horses wouldn't have dragged him away from her in that moment. *Damn!*

Had she realized it? The look on her face when he'd left her told him that it hadn't crossed her mind. Still, he couldn't face her just yet. What would he say? Would she be mad at him? Would she leave? His body heated furiously as the thoughts rampaged his brain.

Delaying the inevitable, he hopped into the shower. The hot water soothed his body but nothing was going to calm his mind right then. He scrubbed hard, as though ridding himself of the stickiness would also rid him of the panic threatening to consume him. He brushed his teeth and combed his hair, not sure whether it was through necessity or cowardice. He really wasn't looking forward to talking to her about what had happened. What *he* had done.

As he pulled on some clean clothes, it occurred to him that she might have already realized the situation and fled. The thought almost made his physically sick and he forgot about fastening his buttons in his hurry to check.

Isla lay curled up on the sofa, sleeping soundly, when he burst through the living room door. She stirred slightly but didn't wake. The warmth of the room soothed him a little and the sight of her tousled curls glinting in the light of the embers took his breath away. Her body glowed in the firelight and he took a quilt from the back of the sofa and wrapped it around her. She smiled without opening her eyes and his heart leaped. She looked so happy and content that there was no way he could wake her just to upset her now. He leaned over and gently kissed her forehead before leaving the room. This was going to take some explaining…

Chapter Thirteen

Isla awoke a while later with a smile on her face and a sticky body. She stretched before snuggling back under the quilt. The fire had sprung back to life and the room was warm and cozy. She really didn't want to move. With a deep sigh, she breathed in the delicious aroma that emanated from the kitchen and realized how hungry she was. It must be almost supper time. The darkness of the room told her it was getting late and she reluctantly hauled herself from the sofa.

"Hey, sleepyhead." Kean was stirring something in a large pan on the stove when she crept up behind him, swathed in the quilt.

"Something smells delicious." She smiled, wrapping one of her arms around him from behind as she peered under his arm at the simmering stew. Her other hand gripped hold of the quilt and her modesty.

"Are you referring to me or the supper?" He turned to face her, raising his eyebrow in question.

She giggled. She loved that look. "Well, actually I was talking about the food, but come to think of it, you're smelling pretty fresh yourself. I see you've showered without me."

He gave a low chuckle. "You, young lady, were dead to the world when I took my shower. Did I wear you out?"

She nodded with a grin. "You could say that." She laughed. "I don't think I've ever slept so well."

"Must be all this country air." He wrapped his arms around her and smiled down, his gorgeous face looking a little less confident than it had earlier.

She nodded slowly with a snicker. "Yeah, that'll be it."

He chortled, holding her a little tighter.

"If you want to grab a shower, I'll have this on the table in ten minutes," he offered.

She feigned shock and indignation. "Are you implying that I smell?"

He laughed. "Darlin', there is nothing at all wrong with your scent. I can promise you that," he said, moving a curl out of her left eye. "In fact, if I had my way, you'd smell like that all the time."

She raised her eyebrows with a smile. "I'm sure that if you had your way, I'd constantly be barefoot and pregnant."

Her frivolity dissipated as she stared into his face. He suddenly looked uncomfortable and her jaw dropped when she realized what the problem was. She took her free hand from around his waist and put it to her mouth.

"Oh no."

He looked panicked as he held her a little tighter and she wondered if he was expecting her to run off.

"Okay, let's think about this rationally," she finally said.

His gaze was pleading with her, but she didn't know in that instance precisely what he wanted from her. That was the trouble. She felt sick as her mind raced, realizing that he had obviously come to terms with the situation before she had even been aware of it. The thought annoyed her a little. Didn't she have a right to know that he'd forgotten the condom?

"I'll go take that shower," she mumbled.

"Supper's in ten minutes. We'll talk…"

She didn't hear the rest of his sentence as she scurried toward the bathroom.

The hot water cascaded over her body and she grabbed a tube of Kean's shower gel to rid herself of the sticky mess. Her hand instinctively lingered on her stomach as she smothered herself in his fresh scent. For a fleeting moment, she imagined a baby growing inside her. The thought didn't fill her with horror as she guessed it should have but with something much different.

Kean had fallen in love with her, as she had with him, regardless of the short time they'd been together. Whatever the outcome of this, it shouldn't change that. And she had never loved anyone more. In fact, she had just come to realize that she had never loved anyone at all, if this feeling was anything to go by. This was so different, so much better than anything she had ever experienced in her life.

With a smile, she ran his shampoo through her hair and felt much fresher when she emerged from the shower. She wrapped a large towel around her and was surprised to bump into Kean right outside the bathroom door.

"Oh."

"Sorry. I only wanted to make sure you were okay." He looked slightly sheepish and she wondered if he had really expected her to disappear. *No way!*

She smiled and he instantly looked relieved.

"I'm fine," she assured him. "Just thought I'd better get some clothes on before that delicious supper goes cold. It smells lovely."

He smiled and her heart melted all over again. Kean was sensitive, despite his alpha-male exterior.

"I'll go and serve up. I've put some clothes on the bed for you."

"Thank you. That's very thoughtful." She stood on tiptoes and kissed his cheek, clearly taking him completely by surprise.

He'd laid out some sweatpants with a T-shirt and sweater, as well as some thick socks. She smiled as she pulled them on.

"Just in time," he said with a grin as soon as she appeared in the kitchen doorway.

She groaned at the tempting aroma that filled the room. It really was heavenly.

"Hope you're hungry." He placed a large plateful in front of her.

"Starving," she admitted.

He sat opposite her and started to eat his meal. "Are you sure you're all right?" he asked after a few minutes.

She nodded. "More than all right." She placed her fork on the table and reached over to lay her hand on his. "Kean, I love you. I meant it when I said it."

It suddenly occurred to her as she studied his face that maybe he had only said it in the throes of passion. Had he actually meant it?

His smile quickly allayed her fears and she relaxed a little.

"I love you, too." He looked a little sad.

"But?" She held her breath.

"But you live on the other side of the state and I live here." He gestured to his surroundings disparagingly.

"So?"

"So I hardly think we're in a position to commute back and forth to see each other, are we?"

She frowned. "Not if you don't want to." She pulled her hand away.

"It's not that." He stared at her in shock. "Isla, you're beautiful and you've got a great career. All that's a million miles away from anythin' I could offer you." He looked so miserable that her heart went out to him.

"I'm not asking you to offer me anything." She spoke softly. "I don't know what's going to happen any more than you do, but I know that whatever happens, we can face it together."

His eyes immediately fell to her stomach and she instinctively put her hand on it.

"We forgot the condom." She thought it was time they addressed the elephant in the room.

He looked surprised and she wondered if it was the word 'we' that had shocked him.

"Yes."

"Okay. So, is it a problem?"

He looked stunned by her question. "Is it to you?"

She smiled. "No."

His face lit up. "Really?" He looked incredulous—

incredulous, but happy.

"Really." She nodded.

He frowned thoughtfully. "Are you on the pill?"

"No."

He nodded slowly, his face clouding over with confusion.

She leaned back in her chair and sighed. "Kean, I love you. We just made love without a condom. If I'm pregnant — and that's a very big *if* — then I'll cope, okay?"

His jaw tightened and his face suddenly looked like thunder. "If you're pregnant then *we'll* cope," he corrected her. "I wasn't lying when I told you I love you, Isla, and this doesn't change anything. We'll take things as they come. Is that all right with you?"

She smiled. His alpha-male side was back.

"Yes, of course." She nodded.

"Good."

They each picked up their forks and resumed their meal.

"This is lovely," she told him.

He shrugged. "It's only Irish stew."

"I wasn't merely referring to the food." She grinned at him, batting her eyelashes playfully and was rewarded by his chuckle.

He gave a knowing nod, making her giggle.

Looking around the room, she thought how comfy it all was. The stove kept it warm and the cushions on the wooden chairs provided a touch of luxury. It was only a small room, but it was all that was needed. It was only a one-bedroom cottage, after all, and clearly suited Kean's needs. She looked toward the window.

"It's stopped snowing," she noted.

"It stopped a few hours ago. It's already started thawing." He looked a little uneasy and her stomach flipped.

"Do you think the traffic will be running tomorrow, then?" She hardly dared ask.

"I'm not sure. I'll put the radio on later and see what the forecast is. I need to go out and see to the horses again after supper, so I'll get a better idea then, anyway."

She nodded, finishing up her food.

The frivolous atmosphere had given way to uncertainty as she pondered the idea of having to leave. She could really get used to living here with Kean.

"I'll wash up," she offered, standing and stacking the plates.

"You're a guest," he reminded her.

"Then I need to earn my keep," she told him with a smile and went over to the sink.

"You don't need to do anythin'," he told her, clearing the rest of the table as she plunged the dishes into the warm, soapy water.

"Are you complaining?" She took a handful of suds and plonked it on his nose, just as he passed her.

"Ha!" He clearly hadn't expected that.

He took the soap from his face and squashed it playfully onto her, dotting it on her cheeks, nose and chin.

"That's not fair! I've got my hands full!" she shrieked gleefully.

"I know." He grinned before putting his hands into the water and taking out an enormous handful of bubbles.

"Oh no. This is too one-sided," she complained with a laugh.

"Are *you* complaining?" He taunted her with the suds, pretending to throw them at her then changing his mind at the last minute.

She laughed, shaking her head. "Don't you dare!"

"Oh, now that's just fightin' talk." He took his other hand and flicked the bubbles at her playfully.

Isla swiped her hand through the suds in the bowl and aimed a big lump of wet mess toward him.

Kean leaped out of the way with a loud guffaw before flicking more of his bubbles at her.

They were both laughing so loud that they almost didn't hear Isla's cell ring from the living room.

"I'll get it." Kean was still giggling as he left the room.

Isla hadn't had so much fun in a long time and she was

still tittering when he came back with the phone. "Just put it on speakerphone while I finish this," she told him, slowly regaining her composure.

"Isla, is that you?" Tabitha's shrill voice cut into the playful atmosphere like a hot knife.

She rolled her eyes. This was typical of her boss to ruin all her fun. "Yes, Tabitha, it's me."

"Good. I've spoken to Mary-Lou Trotter and told her you can't possibly be released to do any more work out there. I've got far too much lined up for you here. She should have realized it was simply a one-off. I told you no good would come of giving her a freebie. I don't know what you were thinking of."

Tabitha's sharp tongue grated on Isla and she had to bite her lip to stop herself from retaliating.

Kean picked up a tea towel and silently began drying the dishes.

"I enjoyed working out here, Tabitha. I've told Mary-Lou I'd be happy to do more shoots for her magazine."

"No. You're under contract with Merchant's. I should never have let you do this job. Poor Stefan's still in hospital, thanks to you." Tabitha was her usual dismissive self, but Isla didn't feel like her usual downtrodden one.

"Stefan is only there under observation and that's more to do with not being able to get transport out of that place," she reminded her boss. "And it wasn't actually my fault. It was an accident. It could have happened to anyone."

"But it didn't happen to just anyone. It happened to one of my best photographers and now I'm short-handed because of it. It's bad enough that you won't be back until tomorrow. I could have done without losing Stefan as well."

Isla felt a lurch in her stomach and she noticed the horrified expression on Kean's face. She frowned.

"Tomorrow?"

"Yes. I'm sending a car over to collect both you and Stefan. You'd better be ready by about half past two. The roads should be relatively passable but Chad thinks he should allow extra time, just in case of delays. He'll pick up Stefan first then go across to the Fielding ranch. Are you in the main house?" Tabitha clearly had it all worked out.

Isla seethed. "No, I'm not at the ranch. I'm at the cottage with Kean Maguire."

There was an uneasy silence as Tabitha clearly digested the news.

"But I thought you were going to the ranch. The Fieldings told me they would be happy to accommodate you." Tabitha sounded terribly annoyed.

"No, we couldn't make it over to the ranch in the snow, so Kean kindly brought me back here. He's been looking after me really well and it's very comforta —"

"Who else is with you?" Tabitha screeched over the phone.

Isla glowed hot with embarrassment and indignation. "No one. He lives alone. Why?"

"Why? Because he's not the kind of man you should be left alone with. That's why." Tabitha sounded furious.

"Tabitha, he's a perfect gentleman," she informed her curtly, trying to quell the anger that was burning in her stomach.

"Perfect gentleman? Ha! You know he only offered to be a guide to impress his bosses, don't you? From what I hear, he's the most sullen, antisocial person around. Trust you to be fooled by him. He's up for some promotion or other, apparently. He obviously thought he'd curry favor with the Fieldings if he volunteered to take you two up the mountain. That's the only reason he did it." Tabitha spat the words out like they were leaving a nasty taste in her mouth.

Kean shifted uncomfortably as she placed the last cup on the drainer, and she immediately regretted having the phone on speaker.

"You don't know anything," she snapped at her boss.

"Actually, it's *you* who doesn't know anything. Don't be taken in by that man, Isla. He hasn't done you any favors."

Isla had just about heard enough. She wiped her hands on her sweater and promptly pressed the button to end the call.

"I'm sorry about her," she told Kean. "I don't know why I put up with her. I really don't."

"Because you feel indebted to her, remember?" His voice was quiet. He quickly finished wiping the last cup and put it in the cupboard above his head. "I need to check on the horses."

Isla guessed that he wouldn't want her company for a while so she watched him get his boots and coat on then head out into the dark. The snow had started to melt already and she could hear it squelching under his feet as he headed for the shed.

She sighed, suddenly feeling irritable and drained. Tabitha Merchant often had this effect on her. When her phone rang again a few minutes later, she immediately geared herself for an almighty row with her boss but was surprised when it was someone else calling her.

"Tabitha tells me you're going back tomorrow," Mary-Lou said.

Isla bit her lip. That was the last thing she wanted to do. "It looks that way," she told her with a sigh.

"I hope you don't mind, dear, but I thought I'd run a feature on you in an upcoming issue of the magazine."

Isla felt a jolt in her stomach. "That's wonderful. I'm very flattered."

"I've got one of my reporters working on the piece already." Mary-Lou sounded a little cagey.

"That's great news." Something told Isla it probably wasn't, but she believed it was the right thing to say, anyhow.

There was a short sigh from the other end of the line. "I spoke to my good friend Beryl Boothroyd about you. I'd simply called to thank her for approaching you about the shoot and to tell her how pleased I am with everything you've done. I showed her some of the pictures, too. I hope you don't mind. She was very impressed."

Isla smiled. "That's good. Of course, I don't mind."

"She told me a little about your past experience. I knew you'd worked for her in a modeling capacity but didn't realize how much work you'd done as a fashion editor."

"Yes, I loved it." Isla recalled how happy she'd been working for Beryl. "I used to do all sorts of stuff on the fashion side of things."

"She told me you were very good at it. Would you consider doing it again?" Mary-Lou sounded a little hesitant.

"In a heartbeat, Mary-Lou. I loved working in fashion and, to be honest, modeling isn't half as glamorous as it's cracked up to be. I'd much rather be back in my old job with Beryl." The thought made her heart ache. Those had been the best days of her life — until now.

"I know you're heading back tomorrow, but do you think you might have time to come to see me before you leave? Providing the weather isn't too bad, of course. I'd like to meet you face to face if it were at all possible."

Isla smiled. "I'd love that," she told her.

"Perhaps we could meet at the office? You could have a look around if you'd like to. See how we operate, maybe?"

"That would be wonderful!" Isla beamed. She already felt like she and Mary-Lou were life-long friends, but that was more because Beryl had told her all about the woman and the magazine before they'd made phone contact. It would be lovely to meet the lady properly.

"Shall we say ten o'clock, then?" Mary-Lou sounded as excited as she was.

"I'll look forward to it," Isla agreed.

Chapter Fourteen

Kean slowly opened the back door. He was surprised to hear Isla chatting away happily and he quietly wiped his boots on the mat. She smiled as soon as she saw him and finished her call, clicking off her cell with a flourish.

He'd been dreading coming back to talk to her after that call with Tabitha, so her change of demeanor totally floored him.

"Hey." She went over and gave him a quick, excited hug.

"I take it that wasn't your boss." He nodded at her cell that she had left on the table.

She giggled. "Yeah, right! No, that was Mary-Lou from the magazine. She wants to meet with me tomorrow."

Kean raised his eyes. "Really?" He wasn't sure of the implications, but Isla sure seemed pleased about it.

"Yep. They want to run a feature on me for the magazine." She helped him off with his coat then took it over to the stove where he unfolded the clothes-horse for her to put it on.

"Great." He frowned thoughtfully. "What about Tabitha?"

He was sorry to have brought up the subject when he saw her face fall.

"She doesn't know. Mary-Lou wants me to go over in the morning. Tabitha said a car will be here about half past two to take me home."

He nodded sadly. He knew it would happen, but hearing it like this just seemed to make it more real somehow.

"So, what did Mary-Lou say?" He followed her through to the living room as they spoke. The lights were off and the fire was throwing shadows up the walls.

"She'd been talking to Beryl Boothroyd again. That's the lady who told her about me. Beryl used to be my boss on the magazine I worked on, *Pretty and Powerful*."

"That was the job you loved so much?"

She nodded, seemingly flattered that he had remembered. "Yes. Beryl told her about the fashion work I used to do on the magazine before I started modeling. Mary-Lou's invited me to go and take a look around her offices. I can't wait to see what it's like." Her face glowed with excitement and shone in the firelight.

"What time do we need to be there?" He switched on a small side lamp and sat on the sofa next to her, holding her in his arms. It felt totally natural to be like this.

"She said about ten o' clock. I can call a cab if—"

"You will not. I'll drive you over to Almondine." He was final about that.

She smiled up at him, her hazel eyes looking almost chocolate-brown in the soft light. He leaned down and kissed her gently on the lips. He was glad he'd given her the sweatpants to wear as they made her feel even softer in his arms.

She stretched a little then settled into his embrace again. "So, how come you're here? I mean, what brought you here from Ireland?"

"A bloody big airplane," he said, making her giggle.

"Duh!" She flashed her eyes at him, cheekily.

"Darling, there's lots you don't know about me," he began, a little nervously. "I came over from Ireland a few years ago with my dad."

"Where is he now?" She looked up at him wide-eyed and he watched her face begin to crumble when she clearly feared the worst.

"He's fine," he assured her, touched at her sensitivity. "He's up in North Dakota. He works for a large agricultural firm up there."

"So, is that what brought you over here? Work, I mean?"

"Sort of. Look, we kind of had to leave Ireland. I'd got

myself into some strife and it was safest all 'round for us to get the hell out of there. Dad managed to land a job out here. I wasn't yet sixteen at the time so I was able to come with him, as a minor. I managed to get into a local school and kept my nose clean until it was time to get a job."

"What did you do for work?" She seemed quite relaxed in his arms and softly stroked his hand that lay across her stomach.

"Whatever I could find." He snickered. "I didn't have many qualifications, if you catch my drift. Never worked hard enough for any of that."

"Why?"

"I'd been too busy gettin' in with the wrong crowd back home. A guy I thought was a friend was actually dealin' in drugs. I wouldn't have anything to do with it, but he kept on at me. Anyhow, one night Dad and me woke up to the Garda — that's the cops over there — banging the hell out of the front door. The bastard McMahon had gone and framed me for some drug deal he had going on. I'd been seen on the street CCTV talkin' with him then some guy had bumped into me as I'd walked away. I'd thought nothing of it at the time, but when they found a packet of the white stuff tucked into the hood of my jacket, I knew exactly how it had got there."

She turned to face him, her face looking pale, even in the darkness. "Oh my God! Did they arrest you?"

He nodded with a grimace. "They did that, all right. Me dad came to the station with me. With me being a minor, he was allowed to stay during the questioning. It was awful."

"But you hadn't done anything wrong," she protested. "Couldn't you just tell them it wasn't anything to do with you?"

He stretched back, running his fingers though her silken hair. She was so naive, so innocent. *So what the hell is she doing with me?*

"It wasn't quite as easy as that," he explained ruefully. He pondered his next move. She had a right to know, even if she walked out on him because of it.

"Isla, I'm not the man you think I am, darlin'."

She turned to face him again, raising her head from his chest. "And who might that be?"

He snickered. "An Irish Cowboy who lives a God-fearin' life in the middle of nowhere."

"You missed the antisocial part," she told him with a cheeky grin. "And wasn't there something about using people to get yourself up the promotional ladder?"

The tense atmosphere immediately lifted and he chuckled, squeezing her gently.

"There's a bit more to it than that, I'm afraid."

She opened her mouth wide, frowning as she feigned horror. "Oh no! What could be worse than that? Should I get my coat now?" She went to move but he held her fast as she giggled.

"You might want to when I've told you, but hear me out first, okay?" He sounded a little more serious and wondered if she realized that her joking about leaving was his greatest fear.

She settled her head back down on his chest, snuggling into him again. They were lying on the sofa now with her slightly on top of him as he held her around the waist.

"I'm all ears," she told him softly.

He took a deep breath. "I used to get bored at school. I bunked off and hung around the town instead of attendin' classes."

"Is that because the work was too hard?"

He was surprised by her question. "No, not at all. Quite the opposite, actually. I was quite good at maths, and English was a doddle. Woodwork and metalwork interested me, so I usually stuck around for those classes, but I had no interest in history or geography."

"It's a pity. It would have come in handy with you traveling," she mused.

"I had no idea I'd ever be goin' anywhere. My parents had both been born and bred in Castlereagh and never left the place. Even when they split up — I was just a baby then — me mam didn't go far. I never saw her, though. She'd gone off with another bloke and had a family with him. Didn't bother about me."

"That's awful."

"Is it? I was quite happy with me dad. He raised me quite well until I hit my teens. Then I heard about other kids at my school whose parents were at war with each other and I started makin' up stuff about my own folks. I suppose I just wanted to fit in — you know, follow the crowd."

She sighed. "I can understand that, I guess."

He shook his head, that sickly feeling returning to his stomach. "I gave me dad hell and he didn't deserve it. I was such a bastard. I started hangin' around with these 'cool kids' down our way and got into all sorts of trouble — fightin', shopliftin', thievin' stupid things just for a bet and stuff like that. It was anythin' to impress the others. I was such a dick." He sighed.

"No, you were a child," she corrected him calmly.

He looked down at her. She was totally accepting of him, not in the least judgmental — and she listened. He'd never been able to talk about this sort of thing before — never wanted to really — because he had no one to tell, apart from his dad and he'd heard enough already.

"So, how did you meet the drug dealer?"

He gave a little smile. Not only was she a good listener but she was also interested in him. He certainly wasn't used to this.

"He was a mate of one of the gang I'd got in with. I thought he was real cool at first. He was older than us, had a flashy car, money, designer gear, the whole package. I wanted a piece of that. He seemed to like me, too, which made me feel flattered — big, you know?"

He sighed again at the memory of how stupid he had been.

"Did he try to get you to sell his drugs for him?" she asked, idly.

"Eventually. It started off with just the odd 'favor'. He'd get me to nick a bottle of whiskey or try to scrounge fags from a pretty shop assistant. Then he wanted me to break into cars and stuff. I refused. Nickin' the odd thing from a shop didn't actually hurt anyone, but I knew how important me dad's car was to him and I thought about what it would do to him if someone stole his wheels."

"Good for you, standing up to him."

He grimaced. "Well, I tried."

"What did he do?" He could hear the tremble in her voice.

"*He* didn't do anythin'. He got his mates to beat me up. I wound up in a hospital because it was so bad. Me dad hit the roof, but I wouldn't tell him what happened. I was too scared. I just said it was a fight that got out of hand, but I know he never believed me." He wound one of her golden curls around his finger as he spoke.

"Did he leave you alone after that?"

"Ha." He sneered. "I wish! No, he just moved it up a gear. If I didn't break into cars for him, he'd do worse to me next time. Anyhow, I went along with it. What choice did I have? But I was shit. Every car's fitted with a damn alarm these days and there was no way I could smash a window, get in and rob anythin' before someone came running after me. I wasn't even the fastest runner, so I ended up gettin' caught more often than not. What me dad had to go through down at the station…" He shook his head in regret.

"But if he knew you were no good at it, why keep making you do it?" She sounded incredulous.

He smiled at her innocence. "Because he was a complete and utter bastard and I was shit-scared of him by then. It gave him a laugh to see me fail — and, of course, I had to take a beatin' each time, which he enjoyed watchin'. He took a shine to this massive BMW that belonged to some executive-guy who worked in one of the big offices in town. He decided I was goin' to break in and steal the car for him."

"Oh no."

He nodded. "I knew I'd never be able to hotwire a car.

Heck, I couldn't even pick a lock! I told him there was no way I could pull it off. Next thing I knew, me dad's car had been stolen and written off. He only had third-party insurance — it was all he could afford — so he lost it completely."

"Oh my God! Did you tell him who did it?"

Bile rose in his throat. "No," he admitted. "I was too scared about what they might do to him next. They knew he was my weak point — my Achilles heel, so to speak. I wasn't goin' to make it any worse. Well, that's what I thought, anyway."

He felt her shake her head next to his chest and knew she was finding all of this hard to take in. Heck, he was struggling to tell her, although that was more because of his own guilt than her reaction. She was wonderful.

"Was that when they tried to frame you for the drugs?" she asked, quietly.

He nodded, though he knew she couldn't see him. "Yes. It was the 'next step up' as he used to put it. Step down, more like. Anyhow, I've never been a fan of drugs. Takin' or dealin', they're just not me. I told him as much when he told me he wanted me to take this package and meet some guy in an alleyway someplace. I wouldn't do it. I couldn't. He got his heavies to beat me up again. Poor Dad nearly had a heart attack when he arrived at the hospital to see the state I was in. He begged me to tell the police who was responsible but I couldn't. I was scared they'd come after him next. I just did what I always did, shrugged and lied."

"You didn't have any choice. You were protecting your dad," she murmured softly into his chest.

He stroked her hair gently. It was good of her to be so supportive. He didn't expect it or deserve it.

"I wasn't long out of hospital when McMahon saw me in the street. He called me over to say how sorry he was and promised it wouldn't happen again — as long as I behaved myself, of course. It was always the same with him. Anyway, when they found the drugs on me, it was the last straw — for me as well as me dad. He'd bailed me out every time and said he just couldn't do it anymore. I had a police record as long as your arm and I wasn't even sixteen yet."

"So, what made you decide to come clean?"

He had a massive lump in his throat and needed to take a deep breath to prevent a sob from escaping. A vision flashed in front of his eyes and he quickly closed them to try to escape it. It was no good. His mind's eye had seen it.

"Me dad cried," he croaked. "I'd never seen him cry before, but he did that day. I couldn't bear it. I told him and the police everythin'. We were moved straight into a safe house while they arrested McMahon and his gang. That's when Dad applied for a transfer to the States through his job. He said if he couldn't stay in his home town then he didn't want to stay in Ireland. It wasn't safe for either of us, anyhow."

"That must have been very hard for him," she said, stirring slightly to look up at him.

Kean nodded. "It broke his heart. *I* broke his heart. He said he understood why I hadn't wanted to snitch on them and he was grateful that I was tryin' to protect him, but I knew I'd hurt him more than anythin' could have. I'd got into that situation myself. With my lies, boasting, showing off…"

"You were a child," she told him firmly, sitting up. "A child from a broken home who went off the rails for a bit, that's all. That doesn't make you a bad person."

He stared at her, stunned. She had been nothing but understanding all evening, but he hadn't expected this reaction. Tears of remorse flooded his eyes and he took an arm from around her to wipe his face with the back of his fist.

"I promised Dad I'd make it up to him," he told her, his voice raspy. "I'm goin' to make him proud of me and I'm goin' to pay him back every penny he had to fork out in fines because of my stupidity."

"You will," she assured him, smiling. "I know you will."

Kean didn't want to let go of her, but he noticed Isla yawning shortly afterward.

"Time for bed," he told her.

She looked up at him through her beautiful long lashes. "Are you planning to join me?"

He grinned. "I thought you'd never ask."

It didn't take long to get ready and they both climbed between the cool sheets, huddling their naked bodies together. Despite the way his cock twitched, Kean knew it was only fair to let Isla get some sleep tonight. She had a long journey ahead of her tomorrow — one which he wished she didn't have to take — and she would need all the rest she could get, especially if she was pregnant. The thought made him hold her a little tighter and he was surprised at how excited he was about the prospect. He had honestly expected Isla to flip when she realized they hadn't used the condom, but she had been fine about it. Actually, she was fine about everything. That was one of the things he loved about her. He felt a warmth as he realized just how much she meant to him.

"I want you to stay," he said aloud into the darkness.

She stirred.

He nuzzled her hair and kissed her head. "I can't bear to think of you leavin' me," he whispered. She must have been asleep already as she didn't say anything, but hearing it made him even more determined. It was ludicrous to think of her miles away doing a job she didn't like in an apartment she hated living in, and maybe even carrying his baby while he was here all alone pining for her — and he knew he would be. Christ, he'd missed her when he was out checking on the horses tonight!

He took a deep breath, smelling his own shampoo on her hair. He was sure she was used to much more expensive designer brands, but he liked the thought of her using his things. It seemed more...intimate.

His brain seemed clearer of its usual fog and he was calm and relaxed for the first time in ages. She certainly had a peaceful influence on him and that could only be a good thing. He wondered what his dad would make of her, and that thought carried him into a dream about weddings and families — and forgiveness.

Chapter Fifteen

Isla awoke in Kean's arms as the sunlight streamed through the open curtains. It sure looked like the snow was going to thaw quickly, and the thought disappointed her. She was nestled into his pounding chest and she moved her head gently to look at him. He was gorgeous. His mouth looked like it was almost smiling, open ever so slightly, showing his perfect teeth. His somnolent eyes looked relaxed and his beard was slightly thicker than usual, but no less attractive. Her heart thumped hard. She loved him. There was no way she could up and leave today. She'd heard him last night, though she hadn't replied, as she didn't know what to say. Making promises she couldn't keep had never been her style, but she had to let him know that she wasn't actually deserting him. She wanted to wake up like this every morning.

Something hard jabbed her stomach and she grinned. She would have given anything to know what was going on in that gorgeous mind of his. Figuring he might need his own space, she carefully slid out of his grasp and threw on his shirt while she went to the bathroom.

The shower was warm and she half hoped Kean would join her. The thought of his hands all over her wet body, caressing and massaging her, was enough to make her wet down below and she smiled as she slid a finger inside herself. Her labia were large and soft and her channel was slick with need as she thrust two, then three fingers into it. The burn in her stomach enticed her to keep going and she didn't stop until she saw bright stars shining in her eyes and had to hold on to the tiled wall to stop herself falling over as she moaned uncontrollably.

In her mind, it had been Kean who had been pounding into her. His face was still in front of her closed eyes as she slowly drifted back to earth. She would never want anyone but him. She loved him. There was no doubt about that.

"Enjoyin' yourself?"

His deep growl permeated her befuddled brain and she jumped around to see him standing outside the shower cubicle, gazing at her. His casual stance, leaning against the wall with his arms folded, suggested he had been there for some time and the fire in his eyes told her he had witnessed everything. *Oh God!*

"I-I...was just coming..." She snagged a towel and wrapped it around her as she stepped out of the shower.

"I could see that." Merriment twitched at his lips while his eyes continued to burn salaciously.

"*Out.* I was just coming *out*," she reiterated, feeling as though her whole body was on fire.

He was only dressed in a small towel slung around his waist and he homed in on her, pinning her against the wall with both her hands above her head.

"Well, that's a shame," he murmured close to her lips. "Because I was rather hopin' to come *in.*"

She stared up into his beautiful face then raised her eyebrows playfully.

"In *you,*" he clarified with a cheeky smile.

Her whole body felt as though it was about to explode as she smiled back at him. There was nothing she wanted more. Silently, she took his hand and led him back under the streaming water, throwing off their towels as they went.

The water was even hotter now that it had run for a while and she relished it on her skin. Kean wasted no time in pulling her into his arms and she was fully aware of his massive erection poised and ready for action.

"We haven't got long," he murmured, nibbling her ear.

She turned to face him then gestured to his massive cock. "I wouldn't say that. It looks more than long enough to me."

She winked at him and he burst out laughing. She loved seeing him happy. His whole face seemed to relax when he smiled and he looked even more gorgeous than ever.

"Is that right?" He hoisted her up and she wrapped her legs around his waist, crossing her ankles behind his back. She wound her arms around his neck and she could feel his cock right up against her as he held her close.

"There's a condom in the cabinet," he whispered close into her ear.

"I think that ship might already have sailed," she reminded him.

"And if it hasn't? Would you want to take that risk?" He looked surprised but not unhappy at her response.

"Judging by the look in your eyes, I'd say I'm taking a risk merely being here with you."

He nodded with a wicked grin. "Ain't that the truth."

"Kean, I want your baby," she murmured, staring into his dark chocolatey eyes.

He gasped and his whole face took on an expression she had never seen before. He looked as though he had just won the lottery. He couldn't have looked happier. There was wonder in his eyes and a massive smile on his lips. "Are you sure?" he breathed.

"Yes. I love you. This is what I want."

He held her closer and as he lowered his lips to hers, his massive cock heaved into her, making her shudder in his arms. The feeling of fullness was one she would never forget and she was almost disappointed when he slowly withdrew only to thrust back in again.

She gripped his body tightly with her legs, enjoying his strength as he held her while pounding hard into her welcoming body.

She stared into his eyes when she felt her orgasm build for the last time and she was about to scream when he crashed his lips onto hers again and she groaned into his mouth. He groaned back, too, thrusting harder than ever as his seed poured into her soaking pussy.

"I love you," she gasped when he finally released her mouth.

"That's funny. I was just about to say the same to you." His eyes twinkled as he panted, and he slowly lowered her legs to the floor, supporting her all the way.

They were still a little breathless when they emerged from the cubicle a short while later, having washed each other down with loving caresses and soft touches that neither ever wanted to end.

"You don't want to be late," he reminded her as he handed her a large bath-sheet.

She sighed. "I'm looking forward to meeting Mary-Lou," she told him. "I don't want to leave you. What will you do? Surely you don't want to look around a magazine office?"

He shook his head. "I don't think I'd ever make one of those male models." He laughed. "I'm sure I can find somethin' to do. Almondine's quite a big place, you know."

She shook her head. "No, I've never been there."

He put his hands to his mouth, feigning shock. "What? You've never been to Almondine? You've not lived, baby! Almondine is the jewel in Cavern County's crown. Didn't you know that?"

She giggled, throwing her wet towel at him. "Then you'd better hurry up and take me to this jewel," she teased.

After she'd dressed and dried her hair, she joined him in the kitchen where he was serving up bacon, eggs and mushrooms.

"You'll need a hearty breakfast. It's goin' to be cold out there," he announced, pointing to the chair where she normally sat at the table.

"Okay, boss," she replied, plunking herself down as instructed.

"Yeah, I like the sound of that," he said, nodding as he dished up her meal.

"This smells heavenly." She was surprised at how much of an appetite she had managed to work up.

After their meal, they went out to see to the horses before

climbing into the truck.

"This is nice," Isla remarked, looking around at the leather upholstery.

"It's not mine. I borrow it from the ranch." He looked a little embarrassed and her heart went out to him.

"Are they good to work for, the Fieldings?" She thought a slight change of subject might help.

He nodded. "Yep, really good. Everyone's real friendly there." He looked at her sideways and grinned. "Despite the rumors about my antisocial behavior, I do actually have quite a few friends."

She giggled. "I don't think you're antisocial," she assured him.

"I'm not the most talkative of guys, I know," he admitted as they drove down toward the town of Pelican's Heath. "I think it's just that I don't want to get with the wrong kind of folk again so I'm a bit wary, that's all. I have to suss out who people are before I decide whether or not to have anythin' to do with them."

"That's understandable. I think you're probably a good judge of character, too, because you take the time to figure people out."

He smiled, much to her relief.

They chatted away about their jobs all the way to Almondine.

"Crikey, it's much bigger than I thought," she marveled as they pulled up in the parking lot.

He nodded. "It's certainly much busier than Pelican's Heath."

"I think I prefer it a bit quieter," she admitted, climbing out of the cab.

Kean came around the front of the truck, his eyebrows raised in surprise. "Says the lady who lives in the city?"

She shook her head. "I told you…it's not out of choice. I'd much rather live out here. It seems more…real, somehow."

He narrowed his eyes as he put an arm around her. "Would you honestly want to move to somewhere like this? I mean, isn't it a bit—I don't know—*plebeian*? Not being rude or anything."

She stopped walking and looked up at him. "You, Kean Maguire, are a snob!"

He shook his head. "I didn't mean it like that. It's just that I thought you were used to the better things in life, if you get what I'm sayin'. Would this be enough for you?"

She gazed into his concerned face, putting her arms around his neck. "Yes, Kean. Anywhere with you would be more than enough." She stood on tiptoes and kissed him gently on the lips, relishing his moan as she did so.

"You are amazin'," he told her when they finally came up for air. "And I love you for it."

She giggled. "Come on. We'll be late if we don't hurry

She needn't have worried as the office building was only around the next corner. It was surprising to see so many shops and offices crammed into the main street, and there was even a large bank at the end of the road. After being holed up in the cottage for the past couple of days and the trailer before that, she had almost forgotten what civilization looked like. She was jostled as she stood on the street, gazing up at the white building, and Kean appeared as though he was about to lay into the woman who bumped her.

"Let's get inside," she said quickly, eager to divert his attention.

With a huff, he consented and they stepped into a cozy little foyer with well-worn but comfy-looking seats and beautiful photographs on the walls. A small reception desk stood at one side and a young woman smiled at them.

"Hello there, I'm—"

"Isla Gillingham!" Recognition crossed the woman's face and she came out from behind the counter, holding out her arms for a hug.

Isla giggled and hugged her back, aware of the surprised look they were receiving from Kean.

"I can't believe you're here. In Almondine. In this office.

I—" The woman gasped.

"I'm here to see Mary-Lou Trotter," Isla explained gently. "She's expecting me at ten."

"Oh…of course you are. I'm so sorry." The lady had turned red with embarrassment and she scurried back around to the other side of the desk. "I'll let her know you've arrived. Please, take a seat." She gestured to the chairs by the door and Isla and Kean went across.

"I'll leave you to it," Kean offered. "You've got my number. Give me a call when you're finished and I'll come to fetch you." He gave her a chaste kiss on the cheek. "I'll see you later. Have fun." He looked over to the woman behind the desk and shook his head incredulously.

Isla giggled. It wasn't often that she was recognized, but she felt a thrill of excitement when it happened. Not that she was famous or anything, but her picture had been in the women's magazines so she supposed some ladies would find her a familiar face.

She sat down as she watched Kean leave. His swagger was so sexy and he was such a gorgeous guy.

"Isla?"

She looked up at suddenly hearing her name.

A lady who must have been in her forties stood smiling in front of her. She was quite plump and wore a fitted suit that beautifully enhanced her curves. Her face was pretty and her bright red lipstick shone in the fluorescent light of the reception area.

"Yes." Isla stood up with a smile, holding out her hand.

"I'm Mary-Lou." Her handshake was as warm as her smile and Isla liked her immediately.

"I know it's not much to look at from out here, but the magazine is really trending upward." Mary-Lou indicated the worn upholstery and threadbare carpet. "I'd like to show you, if you've got the time?"

"Yes, I'd love to see it." Isla followed her, eagerly through a door and into a large office where a huge central desk had been split into four workstations.

"This is where the magic happens." Mary-Lou gestured proudly to the staff members who were working diligently. Three ladies sat at their stations, tapping away on keyboards, and they looked up and smiled as she and Mary-Lou joined them.

"Sarah, Bonnie, Samantha, Raven, I'd like you to meet Isla Gillingham." Mary–Lou presented her and one of the women, who had been standing by the coffee pot, came straight over to them.

"As if you needed an introduction," she said, rolling her eyes at Mary-Lou. "Lovely to meet you, Isla. I'm Raven."

Isla shook her hand with a smile as the other girls rose from their seats and came over to meet her. They were extremely friendly and seemed genuinely pleased to see her there.

At the far end of the table stood a rack full of clothes that caught Isla's eye.

"Are these your new collections?" she asked, gesturing toward them.

"You could say that," Bonnie said with a grimace. "To be honest, they're all a bit of a mess."

"I love that Carhartt on you," Sarah said, spotting Isla's outfit. She had felt a little uneasy about wearing jeans to a meeting with the client but had nothing else to wear, so she'd worn the outfit she'd had for the photo shoot. She smiled.

"It's real comfortable," she told her.

"What about the rest of the outfit?" Mary-Lou narrowed her eyes, obviously guessing that that wasn't the whole story.

Isla smiled. "Do you want the truth?"

"Always. That's how we roll." Mary-Lou smiled but was also clearly bracing herself for some bad news.

Isla bit her lip before continuing. "The cut of the jeans could be a little...different," she offered, as tactfully as she could.

Mary-Lou nodded. "We had to mix up the collection a

little to try to make it work. Guess it didn't, huh?"

Feeling a little uncomfortable, Isla went on "The cashmere sweater is to die for. I'd definitely have a couple of those in my personal wardrobe."

"Samantha picked that one out for you," Mary-Lou explained, and the redhaired girl blushed.

"And I'd never complain about Justin Ropers," Isla said with a giggle.

The ladies all laughed.

"You can't go wrong with a pair of Ropers," Bonnie agreed, as they went over to the rack.

"I'd be interested to get your opinion on some of these garments," Mary-Lou said, gesturing to a couple of tops.

Isla examined them and her heart sank. "These are from suppliers near here?"

Mary-Lou sighed. "Yes. I was hoping to promote a few local businesses. We've had a couple of new factories open up on the industrial estate just outside of town and they want more than a standard advertisement. It could be quite lucrative, only…"

Isla pouted thoughtfully. She spotted a denim skirt with beautiful appliqué flowers splashed across the front. "Wow, I love this." She was hoping that the compliment might cheer up Mary-Lou but it seemed to have the opposite effect.

"It's gorgeous, isn't it? This is from a small independent shop on the main street. Unfortunately, their promotional budget is rather tight as they're only a tiny business, but this is the kind of thing we'd rather feature in the magazine."

Isla checked over the stitching and the hems of the skirt. "You can't beat quality," she remarked, "and I'm afraid this is much better than those." She pointed to the tops that they had initially looked at.

Mary-Lou sighed. "You're right, dear."

"That's the trouble," Sarah interjected. She was a very tall girl with blonde hair piled high on top of her head in a delightful, messy bun. Her make-up was immaculate and her dress screamed class. "The firms with the budgets to advertise are seldom the ones with the garments worth advertising."

"Ain't that the truth?" Raven agreed. "Look at these."

She pulled out a pair of flared jeans with appliqué work along the bottom and running down the side seam. "I know they're a little outlandish, but just look at that needlework."

Isla took the soft denim in her hand. Tiny, delicate butterflies had been appliquéd in a satin material, enhanced with glass beads. Embroidered chains linked them together beautifully.

"I'd wear this," Isla announced.

Silence descended all around her and she looked up to see them all staring at her.

"Really?" Mary-Lou looked hopeful.

She nodded. "Yeah. It's really well-made and it's quirky. I like something a little different, you know? For shoots, I generally have to model the latest trends, but I like to wear more unusual stuff in my own time. I'm guessing these are from the same supplier as this?" She pointed to the denim skirt and the ladies nodded.

"Bretton's," Mary-Lou confirmed.

"But, unfortunately, it's Rowland and Milner who have the bigger budget," Sarah added with a sigh, pulling out the original tops again.

Isla bit her lip again. "So, which collection have you decided on?"

Mary-Lou grimaced, running a hand down the Rowland and Milner tops. "These have the budget to go for a two-page advertisement as well as a three-page feature on the company itself."

"Trouble is that it's nearly impossible to find half a page worth of good things to say about them, let alone three," Bonnie confided. "It's a shame, because a lot of their stuff looks quite good in the photos. It's when you get up close that you notice that the quality's not all there."

Isla couldn't help feeling sorry for the women. Trying to

sound enthusiastic about something that you knew wasn't up to scratch was never easy, but to have to put it in writing must be a nightmare, especially when your name would be at the end of the article. There must be a way to make money to sustain their business while maintaining their good reputation. She just had to think of it.

Chapter Sixteen

"It seems we're caught between a rock and a hard place," Mary-Lou remarked. "Come on. Let's get some coffee and have a proper chat."

"I'll bring some," Bonnie offered and went over to the side counter.

Mary-Lou's office was small and cozy. A large desk stood in front of them, while a small, round table with a couple of easy chairs occupied the space by the large window. Rolls of fabric were propped up against one wall and the desk was strewn with sketches of clothes.

"I'm sure this isn't quite what you expected, dear," Mary-Lou began as they sat down with their hot drinks.

Isla was pleased to notice that they were enjoying their refreshments at the small table away from all the paperwork, as one spill could ruin months of hard work. She'd discovered that the hard way, while working for Beryl.

"I think it's lovely," she replied. "Those ladies seriously care about what they're doing and judging by their appearance, they know all about how to dress and apply makeup. They seem to get along, too. Are they a good team?"

Mary-Lou smiled proudly. "Yes, they all work really well together and come up with some good ideas." She licked her lips thoughtfully. "I definitely want this magazine to go places, you know, Isla? Those girls deserve that much." She took a sip of her coffee.

"I don't see why it shouldn't." Isla nodded.

Mary-Lou sighed. "It was really good of you to agree to

do the shoot for us," she said, a little uneasily. "Having your face in the magazine has already increased pre-orders and sales. We truly are grateful to you."

Isla smiled. "It was my pleasure, honestly. I've loved being out here. It has reminded me of what I've been missing all these years. I was brought up in the country and only live in the city because it's convenient for work. I sort of feel a lot more relaxed out here and I'm beginning to wonder if it was worth moving all that way for. I'm much happier here."

She was surprised at how pleased Mary-Lou looked. "So, you're not really in a hurry to go back?"

Isla grimaced, shaking her head. "Not at all. In fact, I wouldn't even consider returning at all if I wasn't locked into a contract with Merchant's. I mean, I know I need to work, but I've come to realize how much I hate—" She broke off, suddenly remembering that she was actually speaking to a client, not just a friend. "Oh, I'm sorry, I didn't mean..." She put her hand to her mouth, horrified.

Mary-Lou chuckled. "I've heard that Tabitha Merchant can be a real bitch," the older lady confided. "No one in the industry likes her. There's just something not quite right..." She narrowed her eyes thoughtfully as she tapered off.

Isla took a deep breath. "Some of those clothes are beautiful," she said, quickly changing the subject. "I certainly believe you could do a lot with Bretton's."

Mary-Lou took a long sip of her coffee. "And what about Rowland and Milner? They'd be good for business. They could put a lot of work our way and hopefully encourage some of the other factories to advertise with us."

Isla pursed her lips. She sat forward in her seat, placing the coffee cup back on the table. "Okay, here's what I think. Bretton's is good quality. They could be a trendsetter. Their stuff is new, different, and I'm sure with the right advertising, they could go a long way. If *Country Girl Magazine* were instrumental in their success, it can only be good for you guys. Other companies will sit up and take notice. It'd put you on the map, so to speak."

She leaned back in her chair. "Mary-Lou, you've got to consider your reputation. This is a high-class magazine. You need your advertisements to reflect that. Features and articles about new, innovative companies are your way forward. You can include lower-end companies by way of comparison. It's good to have some kind of budget-conscious stuff to contrast with the high-end, but you shouldn't only concentrate on the companies who can offer you more work if they're not the ones that will grow your own business."

Mary-Lou's eyes lit up, and Isla guessed she'd had a 'light bulb moment'. "You're right, dear," she said.

"Does Bretton's want to work with the magazine?" Isla asked, taking a sip of her drink.

Mary-Lou nodded. "Oh yes, definitely. They were only too happy to be approached and wanted to do all sorts of features with us. They need to raise their profile, especially now that the new industrial estate's recently been built with multi-national companies taking up factory space. The independent stores are worried sick that they'll go out of business as people will go to where they can get more variety and get it cheaper. You know how these things work. We've got several small shops set to close in the near future if things continue like this."

"The ethos of your magazine is to sustain small businesses and help them grow, isn't it?" Isla had read their mission statement the previous night when she had researched the magazine in preparation for today's meeting.

Mary-Lou seemed impressed, as she nodded. "Yes. The only trouble is that they simply don't have the advertising budgets that these big conglomerates have. Unfortunately, we need to sustain the magazine as well as promote traditional values. It's not easy to do both."

"Nothing worthwhile is ever easy," Isla reminded her. "Bretton's needs a leg up then their brand will sell itself, in my opinion. I really think your magazine should be a part of that success."

Mary-Lou frowned. "We can't afford to give away free advertising, though, Isla, much as I'd like to. I know you gave up your time for free, but—"

"And I can do it again," she interjected. "Or"—she thought for a moment—"once Bretton's get advertising in your magazine, I'm sure their sales will rocket, especially if they're selling via the Internet. How about doing some promotion for them and letting them pay in, say…three months' time? That should enable them to make some money to pay you back and keep your accounts team happy because the money will be coming in under contract."

"That could work," Mary-Lou agreed, licking her lips thoughtfully. "But I wouldn't be able to spend too much time on their campaign when I've got other clients who are paying upfront. It wouldn't be fair, and, besides, I seriously need to concentrate on keeping the revenue coming in to keep the magazine running smoothly."

Isla sighed. "It's such a shame I have to go back today," she said. "I would love to go and see Bretton's for myself. I wouldn't mind doing a photo shoot with some of their clothes. I'd enjoy that."

"It's very kind of you, dear, but you know Tabitha Merchant won't allow you to stay any longer than is necessary, and—"

The phone interrupted Mary-Lou's protestations and she frowned as she lifted the receiver. "Bonnie, I thought I told you that I— Oh." She looked surprised. "All right. Yes, of course, send her straight in." She replaced the receiver.

"I can go if—" Isla offered, getting up.

Mary-Lou shook her head, gesturing for her to sit back down. "No, I think you might want to stay for this. Someone's dying to see you again, anyhow."

The door burst open and Beryl Boothroyd strutted in, closely followed by a very apologetic-looking Bonnie.

"Isla!"

She shot to her feet and ran to give her friend a hug.

Beryl was a very large woman with a booming voice and personality to match. She commanded every room she entered, and this was no exception.

"What brings you here?" Mary-Lou asked, pulling out a chair for her guest.

"News." Beryl looked very secretive as she slowly undid her silk Hermes scarf and unbuttoned her fur coat.

Bonnie placed a cup of coffee in front of her before scurrying off.

"Well, I hope it's *good* news. Isla's due to go back this afternoon and I need her here," Mary-Lou replied, matter-of-factly.

Beryl raised her eyebrows. "Is she going to help you out again?" She smiled conspiratorially.

"I won't allow her to work for nothing, but she's got some great ideas about how to get us on the map *and* help our local businesses." Mary-Lou was clearly impressed, and Isla beamed with pride.

Beryl winked at her. "I taught her well," she replied.

Mary-Lou rolled her eyes. "It's a pity you've retired. We could do with you helping out around here. I've got a feeling things might get really busy if everything works out the way I'm thinking."

Beryl leaned back in her chair, smiling. "I'm too busy enjoying a life of luxury, sticking my nose in everyone else's business."

"Well, you could always invest in the magazine," Isla suggested. "You could take on a sort of consultant's role."

Mary-Lou grinned and turned back to Beryl with a questioning look.

"Ha-ha!" Beryl laughed. "I might do that, sweetheart," she said, staring at Isla.

"So, what's this news you've brought that's worth interrupting our meeting for?" Mary-Lou asked her with a cheeky grin.

Beryl rolled her eyes. "Okay, strap in, girls." She sat forward in her chair and they all huddled toward her, conspiratorially. She looked over at them. "Crikey, we look like the Bitches of Eastwick," she declared with a loud guffaw.

Isla smiled. Beryl always was such fun to be with, and she missed her terribly.

"Just get on with it," Mary-Lou told her with a tut.

"Right, well, here's the thing." Beryl looked very excited. "You know *Beauty Personified* was doing really well then all of a sudden we heard it had gone bankrupt?" Isla nodded, remembering it only too well. "The rumor that went around at the time was that Philip Coffey, the owner, had embezzled the money from the company and used it for his own means."

"Yeah, but he'd disappeared, so it couldn't be proved," Isla interjected ruefully.

"Well, guess what? Behind every wayward man there's a conniving woman. And in this case, you'll never guess who his girlfriend was?" Beryl's eyes were wide as she waited for the penny to drop.

Isla put her hands to her mouth. "No."

Beryl nodded. "None other than Tabitha Merchant."

"That certainly explains how Merchant's Models suddenly became successful after the magazine went out of business," Mary-Lou said, thoughtfully.

"They were lovers. But when the money ran out, Tabitha left him but took most of the money. Coffey had an ally, Ralph Winston. You know, the guy who owns the Winston Hotel chain? Well, he bailed Coffey out once the cops had caught up with him and got his legal team to lessen his prison sentence to just a few months. Now that he's been released, he's baying for blood. I've got a lawyer-friend who had a word with a certain attorney the other night after they'd had too many drinks. The attorney happened to be working on a case for Philip Coffey, who, by the way, is about to sue the ass off Tabitha Merchant. In fact" — she checked her watch — "Tabitha should be receiving the news any time now."

Isla stared at her friend, stunned. "But that means Merchant's will fold, surely?"

Beryl nodded. "Exactly. Which means you, young lady, will have to think about looking for another job."

Isla's stomach lurched and her breathing quickened. "So I'll be released from my contract?"

"Of course. I take it you don't want to work for Tabitha anymore?"

"Nope. I want to stay out here, in Cavern County."

"Perhaps working on a small fashion magazine?" Mary-Lou asked with a mischievous smile.

"Could I? I mean...would you take me on? I'd love to work here." The words were a little breathless as excitement and hope welled inside her.

"I could do with a right-hand woman and you've got some great ideas. I'm not sure if the wages would match what you're used to, but as soon as the magazine grows, your paycheck will, too." Mary-Lou looked a little hesitant.

"That's perfect! I'd love to!"

They all stood up and hugged the breath out of each other, giggling and gasping.

Isla glanced at the clock on the wall. It was already ten past twelve.

"I need to call Tabitha and tell her not to send the car. I don't need it now," she said, pulling out her cell that she'd muted for the meeting.

She frowned, noticing a message. "Tabitha left a text saying that something's come up at the office. She hasn't been able to send transport."

Beryl smiled. "She's probably had all her assets seized while they look into her financial records. If she's built up her business on stolen money, there's no way they're going to let her continue trading while they investigate it."

"But she hasn't said I'm out of a job or anything." Isla's mind whirled.

"Don't worry about it and don't jump ship. As far as you're concerned, you're merely waiting to go home and get back to work. She doesn't need to know you're aware of her dirty secret or that you've got another job lined up." Beryl smirked. "Karma's a wonderful thing, don't you think?"

* * * *

By the time Isla went to find Kean, she was floating on air. Everything seemed totally surreal. They met up at a small coffee shop not far down a side street. It was cozy and she stood in the doorway looking around for him. He sat at the far side of the room by the window. She frowned. He was gazing out the window with a far-away look in his eyes. His shoulders sagged and he looked like he was carrying the weight of the world on them. He smiled when he caught sight of her, but he still appeared melancholy.

She rushed over to him and flung her arms around his neck. "I love you so much," she whispered. "And I've got some good news."

He looked up at her in surprise. "Well, I can't wait to hear it, darlin'. Let me just get you some tea. Or would you rather have coffee? They do a mean latte — or so I've been told."

She glanced at the table and saw a little brown teapot next to his cup. "I'll have tea, thank you. I seem to have gotten quite a taste for it lately."

He summoned a waitress while she slid into the seat opposite him.

"Were you bored? I'm sorry I was so long. Loads has happened, though. I'm dying to tell you." She bubbled with excitement.

"No, not at all. I went around the shops. Caught up with a couple of mates and had a drink, then came back here to wait for you. It's been a pretty chilled day, if I'm honest."

"Good. You don't seem all that happy though." She leaned forward and took hold of his hands across the table. "Is everything all right?"

He nodded. "Of course. I've been thinkin' about how

much I wish you didn't have to go back today. I don't know when we'll see each other again, but, God, I hope it's not too long. I missed you in just the couple of hours you were in your meetin', I honestly don't know how I'll cope for weeks or even months apart."

He blinked hard and she guessed he was close to tears.

"I'm not going back today – if ever."

They drank their tea while she explained the whole situation. Kean spent most of the time with his mouth wide open as he took it all in and his jaw must have been aching like mad by the time she'd finished.

"So you won't be tied into your contract? You'll be free to leave Merchant's?"

"Yes, but I won't just leave. I'll have to wait until she tells me I'm out of a job, otherwise I can still be accused of breaking the contract."

He grinned, getting up from his seat. She quickly stood and they shared a massive hug, right there in the middle of the coffee shop.

"Of course, if I'm going to be working at *Country Girl Magazine*, I'll need somewhere to live close by. Can you think of anywhere?" She batted her eyelashes at him cheekily.

"Too damn right, I can. Mind you, it'll only be until we find somewhere a bit bigger. I've got a feelin' we're goin' to need more than one bedroom if this mornin's anythin' to go by." He winked, reminding her of their antics in the shower. She beamed.

"I meant what I said," she told him. "I want to have a family with you. You can keep me barefoot and pregnant as long as you like."

"Good. 'Cause I intend to. There's just one other thing."

She gasped as he got down on one knee in front of her – and in front of all the rest of the customers. She put her hands to her mouth, not daring to hope for what she really wanted him to be doing.

"I wouldn't *exactly* call this place the jewel in Cavern

County's crown, but it does have a great jeweler's shop. I popped in earlier and this caught my eye. I thought you might like it."

He looked sheepish as he handed her a small red velvet box and her fingers trembled as she clutched it.

"I'll get you a much better one when I'm a bit more flush, of course, but I wanted you to have something to take away with you, to remember me by. Not that you need to now, of course – or at least I hope not."

She giggled as he rambled on, taking in every word, memorizing this moment until it was imprinted on her brain.

He shook his head with a snicker when he caught her expression. He rolled his eyes. "Well, I should have the gift of the blarney, I suppose, being Irish, so you'll have to excuse me going on. What I'm trying to say is" – he slowly opened the box in her hand – "will you do me the honor of becoming my wife?"

A tiny diamond solitaire winked at her from the plush box before it all went blurry as tears streamed down her hot cheeks.

"Yes," she whispered, nodding. "Yes, please. I'd love to marry you, Kean." She sniffed hard as he took the ring from the box and slid it onto the finger of her left hand.

"Thank you," he whispered, slowly standing and taking her in his arms. There were cheers and hoots all around them as she held him each other, never wanting to let go.

Isla was overwhelmed as she tried to accept what was happening. For once in her life, everything was perfect. She couldn't wish for more.

Chapter Seventeen

"Where to next?" Kean didn't think he'd ever stop smiling. Isla loved him and wanted to marry him. It was a dream come true.

He looked over at her as she elegantly rose from her seat and they left the coffee house to raucous applause. She looked positively radiant.

"Aren't you in a hurry to get back to work?" She looked at him a little quizzically as they walked up the street. She kept holding out her hand to admire her ring.

"No. I'm lookin' after the client, remember?" he teased.

She giggled. "There is one shop I wouldn't mind going to if it's okay? I don't know exactly where it is. It's called Bretton's."

He raised his eyebrows. "Bretton's Boutique? Yeah, I know it. Come on."

His arm was around her as they marched up the busy street. He noticed she was still gazing at her ring.

"I'll get you a better one later," he promised. "One with a proper diamond in it, not just a wee chip like that. And maybe a more decorative band."

"You will not. I love this ring, Kean Maguire, and I love the man who gave it to me. I wouldn't change a thing."

She looked so beautiful but firm as she gazed up at him in amazement, and he stared back at her.

"Surely you'd like one a bit better than that, though?" He had felt a little embarrassed that he couldn't afford more right now, but he was determined to make things better for her. When he had gone into the jeweler's, he had been afraid he might not see her again for months. He'd been determined to give her something to remind her of him, something that would remind her how much he loved her. He grimaced. That ring was hardly a good representation of the way he felt about her. Far from it.

She shook her head, sending those curls of hers into a spin. "I don't want another one, Kean. This one is perfect."

The sincerity in her face and determination in her voice made him bend down and take her lips in a slow, soft kiss. He teased her tongue with his, before giving it a friendly nip, which made her giggle. He loved that sound so much.

"This is it." They stood outside the boutique. Brightly colored clothes and bags adorned the window. He had often thought it was quite cheerful to look at but had never had cause to venture inside.

"Brilliant."

He followed her in, failing to see what was brilliant about it, but as long as she was happy, he was happy, too. He smiled as he saw her face light up when she gazed at all the clothes. Her ring glinted in the bright lights as she ran her hand over some soft-looking fabrics and he couldn't help considering how beautiful she would be in a long, white dress.

"What do you think of these?" Her excited voice cut into his thoughts and he balked at the sight of the pale blue jeans with fancy embroidery all down the outer seams. He had to admit that they looked really pretty, but he was surprised that she would be interested in anything so bright. He'd seen some pictures of her in a few magazines the hands had brought into work when they'd heard she was coming to Pelican's Heath, and in every one, she wore plain or classic styles.

She didn't wait for his reply. "I'm going to try them on," she announced. She also picked out a pretty white top that had just a little white embroidery on the yoke.

He hung back as she spoke to the assistant who showed her into a dressing room. While he waited, he took a good look around the shop and was surprised to find himself admiring the outfits. Although a lot of the items had gaudy patterns or intricate embroidery on them, there were a few things that looked a little more refined. Blouses with floaty, feminine sleeves hung on one rack, while skirts with flowers and animals sewn onto them hung on another. There were lots of pairs of jeans adorned with different patterns and even some cute satin slippers with embroidery and beads across the top.

"What do you think?"

He looked up on hearing her voice and had to catch his breath. The bright colors in the embroidery of her jeans contrasted beautifully with the plain white cotton of her top, while the stitching on the yoke brought the whole outfit together. She certainly had a good eye for fashion.

"Fantastic," he uttered, suddenly realizing he hadn't replied yet.

She beamed at him. "Good."

He smiled to himself as she disappeared into the cubicle again and noticed the owner, Alexander Bretton, come through from the back of the shop. The young assistant whispered something to him and he beamed. He was a very tall, slim guy with a great sense of style. His own clothes were quite classic, but Kean had heard that there was always something unusual about his outfit—a bright colored handkerchief poking out of a pocket or a patterned pair of socks. He obviously liked to stand out in a crowd, and it was a credit to him.

Isla emerged from the dressing room, holding the clothes. "I'm just going to look around a little more," she told the assistant.

Alexander Bretton took a step toward her. "Miss Gillingham, isn't it?"

She smiled at him. "It is."

"Alexander Bretton." He held out his hand and she shook it politely.

"Mr. Bretton, I love your shop. May I introduce my fiancé, Kean Maguire?" She beamed as she nodded to him, gesturing for him to come forward.

Kean felt ten feet tall. *Fiancé*. It sounded so strange and yet so right—though not as right as 'husband', he thought with an inward glow. "Hello, it's good to meet you." He nodded as they shook hands.

"Nice to meet you, too, Mr. Maguire. And may I thank you for bringing your fiancée here." Mr. Bretton smiled, gesturing to his shop.

"Your clothes are beautiful and the quality is superb." Isla had spoken before Kean had the chance to explain that it was, in fact, *her* idea to come here, not his.

Mr. Bretton's smile almost split his face in two. "I'm glad you think so, Miss Gillingham."

She nodded. "It's Isla, actually. I'm looking for something smart, if you have anything. Not too stuffy, but not as casual as those." She gestured to the outfit that she had placed on the counter.

"For yourself?"

She smiled. "Yes."

He could hardly contain his excitement and Kean watched in amusement. In the fashion world, Isla Gillingham really was somebody, and these people seemed to worship at her feet. He felt even more proud to be the one who was with her.

She winked at him as she let the owner lead her over to a rack by the far wall. She picked up a straight, gray skirt that had a touch of white embroidery embellishing the side seams. "I love this look," she told the guy. "Is there a white blouse I could put with it? Nothing too stark. Maybe a soft chiffon or something? I'd like it to drape here."

Kean loved to see her enjoying herself. He could tell that she would fit right in at the magazine and he was sure everyone in Cavern County would love her. His heart leaped at the thought that she was going to stay with him. Marry him. Have his…

A vision of her with a baby in her arms flashed through his mind and he swallowed a hard lump in his throat. She wanted to have a baby. *His* baby. What more could she give him? What more could he want?

He watched in awe as she gathered together a few more items, including some underwear, he noted, and even a pair of red shoes — again with the signature embroidery across the front — and she made her way back to the counter. Kean so wanted to intercept her and offer to pay, but he couldn't, not after paying for the ring. The thought made him feel sick.

"You're actually going to wear these yourself?" Alexander Bretton gushed over her as she handed the assistant her card.

"Yes, of course."

The young girl put them into a large bag for her.

"Don't be surprised if you see them popping up on social media and the like," Isla added with a wink. "I intend to wear the hell out of them, crediting Bretton's, of course."

"We'd be grateful for any publicity, Miss Gillingham. We're only a small business and we're striving for a place in today's busy marketplace."

"You do mail order, too, don't you?" she said, thoughtfully.

He nodded.

"Do you have any advertising material with your website on it or anything?" She looked around the counter.

"Well…er…no, not as such. But I can write down the address of the website for you," he offered eagerly.

She pursed her lips then peered at the brown bag the assistant had put her purchases into. It had the name of the shop emblazoned across the front.

"It's okay, I'll find it. I can simply google the shop, can't I?"

"Yes."

"You might think about getting the website address written on the bags," she said, thoughtfully. "And maybe a logo or something. Anything to make you stand out. Your fashions are bright and colorful — maybe your bags should be, too."

Bretton frowned thoughtfully. "I hadn't thought of that. You might be right." He nodded.

"I hope you're not offended or anything. I just came from a marketing meeting and I'm all fired up to take on the world," she said with a self-deprecating smile.

"Any ideas you have would be most welcome, Miss Gillingham. You know the market better than most, and I welcome your help."

She smiled at him. "That's good. You might be seeing quite a bit more of me from now on."

His face could have lit up the Golden Gate bridge. "I'll look forward to it," he assured her.

Kean took her bag from her and threw a possessive arm around her shoulder as he led her out of the shop.

"I think you made his day," he told her before kissing her hair.

"You made mine." She stopped and turned to smile at him, gazing up though her long lashes. "I love you."

He bent down to take her lips in a lingering kiss, his heart thumping like a drum. "I liked bein' called your fiancé," he murmured afterward.

"I liked calling you it." She beamed. "It's got a nice ring to it." She held up her hand, "Actually it's got a *beautiful* ring to it."

The tiny diamond sparkled in the winter sun.

"I'm still goin' to get you a better one," he promised.

"You can't replace this one," she insisted. "It's perfect."

They kissed again before being jostled as they stood in the busy street.

"Anywhere else you want to go?" he asked, freeing her mouth much sooner than he would have liked.

"I'm all done. Don't you think you should be getting to work, though? I'd like to meet the Fieldings, anyhow."

"Slave driver," he muttered, shaking his head teasingly. "Come on then."

He loved the way she held him tightly as they made their way back to the truck. The paths were riddled with puddles

167

of melting snow and the sun was brighter than it had been in days.

"Hello." They were suddenly stopped by a young woman who stared at Isla. "You're Isla Gillingham, aren't you?"

Isla nodded with a smile. "I am."

"Please, could I have your autograph? I love your work." The girl was definitely star-struck, and Kean grinned as Isla scribbled her name on the back of an old envelope the fan had pulled from her bag.

He was surprised when the stranger then gave Isla a hug and took a selfie with her before letting her go.

"Does that happen a lot?" He asked when they finally said good-bye to the woman and crossed over to the parking lot.

"Not really," Isla replied, looking slightly embarrassed. "Is it a problem?"

"As long as it's just the women," he grumbled.

She stared at him, open-mouthed, at the door of the truck. "Seriously? Kean Maguire, I do believe you're jealous."

He was about to object but on reflection realized that she was actually spot-on. "Yeah, well, who can blame me?" he admitted.

"You know you're the only man I want," she said with a sympathetic smile.

"Right answer." He nodded as he smiled back at her and took her lips for one more kiss before they both climbed into the truck.

Isla admired her ring all the way to Pelican's Heath. He was relieved and happy that she loved it so much.

"I want to give you the world," he told her softly.

"*You're* my world," she replied, placing her hand on his thigh.

The warmth that glowed inside him whenever she was near became a burn, and he wished he wasn't driving so he could take her in his arms again. Instead, he placed his hand on hers and smiled.

"I've been looking forward to seeing where you work," she said, looking out the window eagerly as they pulled up at the ranch. "This place is wonderful."

Kean parked the truck and quickly went around to open her door for her. It was early afternoon and he knew most of the hands would be having their lunch and therefore would be out of sight in the staff room.

Isla climbed elegantly down from the truck, her hand holding his tightly, and she smiled as she looked around at the rows of stables and the large training paddock that stood in front of the main house.

"Hey there." Aidan Fielding came over from one of the stables, smiling.

Kean's stomach jolted. He knew his bosses had doubted his capabilities of handling the visit and wondered just what crap had been said about him in his absence. The fact that the boss had a massive grin on his face could be a good sign—although he *was* looking straight at Isla.

"Isla Gillingham, please meet my boss, Aidan Fielding," he offered politely.

"I hope he's been looking after you?" Aidan inquired, still grinning.

"Oh, he has, sir. He's been wonderful," she assured him.

"Great. Why don't you two come on up to the house? There's hot coffee and I'm sure I smelled chocolate cake baking earlier."

Kean felt a little sick. The only times he was invited into the house was when there was something important to discuss. And his instinct told him that this time it involved Tabitha Merchant.

Chapter Eighteen

Isla smiled as she sat in the big, warm living room of the Fielding ranch house. A big fire roared in the grate and the furniture was soft and homey. Kean sat next to her on the huge sofa, while Aidan went to see about refreshments.

"You look worried," she whispered. "Are you okay?" She held his hand tightly.

"Yeah, I just—"

"Hello, I'm so happy to meet you." Kean was interrupted by a very excited young lady who rushed in, wiping her hands in her apron. "I'm Josie."

Isla took her hand with a smile. "Hi, Josie, I'm Isla." She noticed a couple of scratches on her hostess's face.

"I know." Josie shook her head, beaming. "I simply can't believe you're here…in my house. It's so wonderful."

"Well, thank you for having me." Isla nodded graciously. "You have a beautiful home. And we have matching injuries." She pointed to her own cheek. "Are you all right? Mine was a rock, but it's okay."

"Oh, no. Mine was a car, but I'm fine, too."

Aidan arrived with a large tray that he placed on the coffee table in front of them. He rolled his eyes. "Come on, Josie. How about some of this coffee? My mouth's as dry as a parrot's cage."

Josie quickly looked around and nodded. "Of course. Do you take sugar, Isla?"

"No, thank you." Isla smiled, blushing slightly. She wasn't used to people clamoring over her. She wasn't exactly a celebrity or anything. And she was surprised that the people of Cavern County had actually heard of her, being as she did most of her work in the city.

"You have to excuse my sister," Aidan said, shaking his head. "She gets a little…*excited* sometimes."

Josie gaped at her brother. "It's not every day we get someone like Isla Gillingham in our house," she reminded him. "This is a once-in-a-lifetime occurrence. I want to make the most of it."

"You're right about that," Aidan teased her. "She'll never want to come again with you gushing all over her like that."

Josie narrowed her eyes at her brother as she poured out the coffee in silence. Isla couldn't help feeling sorry for her. She looked so disappointed.

"Well, if that chocolate cake tastes half as good as it smells, you won't be able to keep me away," she said as she took her cup.

Josie's eyes lit up. "I hope you like it," she said, as Aidan passed over a slice.

"Who doesn't like chocolate cake?" Isla beamed as she placed her cup on the small side table and took the plate and fork.

She felt everyone's eyes on her as she took the first mouthful. It was blissful.

"That is the best chocolate I've ever tasted," she said with a nod. She meant it. The cake was perfectly light and the chocolate was strong without being bitter. It had exactly the right amount of cream in proportion to the sponge, and Isla moaned with delight as she took another mouthful.

"Does that mean you'll come again?" Josie asked eagerly.

"Give the girl a chance," Aidan said with a laugh, as they all settled down with their coffee and cake. "She lives in the city, remember? She can't exactly pop in for coffee whenever she feels like it, now, can she?"

Josie looked crestfallen. "I suppose not."

"Actually, I'm planning to stick around," Isla told them.

Josie's face shone. "Really?"

Isla held up her hand to show them her ring. "Kean and I are getting married." She felt him squeeze her other hand

and looked over to see him glowing with pride.

Aidan was on his feet in a second. "Well, dang it! That was quick. Congratulations, both of you. I'm real happy for you." He shook Kean's hand and gave Isla a warm hug.

"I can't believe it. You're going to live around here?" Josie held Isla tightly.

"Yep, I'm going to move in with Kean," Isla told her, smiling.

Aidan looked surprised. "In that old shack? There's hardly room to swing a cat."

"We're not getting a cat," Kean mumbled.

"Did we miss something?" A man with dark hair walked in, closely followed by another couple of men and woman.

"Hell, yeah. Kean's getting married — to Isla Gillingham," Aidan announced. "They've got the ring and everything."

"Ooh, let's see." A plumpish woman with a big smile pushed past the men to come and examine the rock on Isla's finger.

"That's beautiful," she said, "classy and understated. I love that. I'm Maggie, by the way." She smiled and gave Isla a quick hug. "Aidan's wife."

"Lovely to meet you, Maggie."

"And this here's my brother Ben, and that's Cordell and Jarrod," Aidan explained.

Isla noted that people around here seemed to prefer hugging to shaking hands, and that was fine with her. She felt welcomed by everyone and had a terrific sense of belonging, even though she hadn't been there long.

"I'll send some hands up to fetch those horses down later," Cordell told Kean, shaking his hand to congratulate him.

"No problem. They're in the large shed, all fed and watered," Kean replied. He turned to Isla. "Cordell's the foreman," he explained.

"I'm sorry for detaining him this morning," she said. "I needed to get into town and Kean offered to drive me. I hope that was all right with you." She felt a little guilty and wondered if Kean was in any trouble for missing work.

"That's no trouble at all," Cordell assured her. "It was part of his job, actually, to look after the client."

"We would have had you over here, you know?" Ben reminded her.

"Kean looked after me real well. I was just fine where I was, thank you," she told him with a smile.

Ben looked at her ring with a grin. "Yeah, I see that."

They all laughed and Josie offered refreshments as they sat down.

"Here, let me help with that," Maggie offered. "You're supposed to be resting, remember?"

"I'm glad you told her that, darlin'. She won't listen to me." Aiden rolled his eyes.

"I'm fine, honestly. Besides, I didn't want to miss out on meeting Isla, did I?" Josie smiled, but Isla wondered just how badly she'd been hit by that car. Didn't Kean mention that she'd been in hospital?

"I heard about the accident up on the mountain. You must have been terrified," Maggie remarked, sitting opposite them, next to Aidan.

"I was," Isla admitted. "I was in total panic — shock, you know? Luckily Kean knew exactly what to do. He called the medics and kept me and the horses safe. They took Stefan to the hospital, but he's okay. A broken leg, I think, but he's going home today."

Ben nodded. "We sent someone over to drive him."

Kean gaped. "*You* did?" He and Isla exchanged a look. Things must be awfully bad back at the office if they hadn't even managed to arrange transport for Stefan. After all, he could hardly hop on a train like Isla, could he?

"There was some mix-up at his work, I believe. He rang here to speak to Isla as he couldn't get her on her cell, and when he explained, I sent one of the hands over to drive him back home." He shrugged, tucking into his cake.

Isla frowned and pulled her cell from her back pocket. Sure enough, there was a missed call from Stefan. *Damn.*

She'd forgotten that her phone was muted for the meeting and she hadn't switched the ringer back on. "That was real nice of you," she told him, touched at the gesture.

Ben looked surprised. "It's what we do." He shrugged again, resuming his cake.

Isla snuggled into Kean's arm. *It's what country folk do,* she thought, looking forward to being part of such a caring community.

"Shame about his accident," Aidan remarked. "I heard he tripped over his own equipment."

"That's right," Kean replied guardedly.

"Don't look so worried," Ben said with a grin. "He told us all about it. You're his hero, apparently. He thought he was a goner when he fell off that cliff. Typical city boy. You weren't even that high up, from what I heard, and with all that brush beneath you, he would've had quite a soft landing."

"It *was* scary," Isla insisted, a little defensively.

"Yeah, I guess so," Ben relented. "And he hadn't known about the snow, of course. He'd been quite worried at the thought of you guys having to bring three horses down in that weather."

"It wasn't that bad," Kean replied.

"Bad enough," Cordell interjected.

"Yeah, it was a good thing you had the sense to keep in touch," Aidan added. "We were contemplating sending out help."

Kean shook his head. "There was no need for any of that," he assured them.

"Stefan said he'd taken some incredible photos," Ben commented.

Kean frowned at him. "You did have a good old chat with him, didn't you, boss?"

Ben chuckled. "He was a client. I had to make sure he was happy, especially after..."

Kean stiffened beside her.

"After what?" His voice was deep and he spoke slowly.

Her heart hammered painfully against her chest.

"Well, we met Tabitha Merchant, as you know," Ben went on, shaking his head. "What a strange woman. Oh…I'm sorry." He looked apologetically at Isla.

"Oh no, it's fine," she assured him. "Strange is a good word for her."

Ben snorted. "I could certainly think of a few more, but I couldn't repeat them in company," he confided.

"Couldn't we all?" Isla rolled her eyes.

"So you don't get along with her too well, I take it?" Ben looked intrigued.

Isla shook her head. "She's professional and very good at her job," she explained, "but she's not what you'd call a 'people person', you know?"

"There's a few of them about," Jarrod interjected, smirking at Kean.

"Actually, I think we might have misjudged this guy," Ben said seriously, wagging a finger at Jarrod. He turned back to Kean, who shifted a little uncomfortably.

"Ms. Merchant wasn't exactly complimentary, as I'm sure you'd have guessed, but when we spoke to the other guys, we got a completely different story."

"We sure did," Aidan chimed in, smiling.

"Chad said you were very polite," Ben went on, "and that you handled Ms. Merchant beautifully." He frowned. "He didn't exactly go into detail, but I caught his drift."

Isla stifled a giggle, remembering the incident he would have been referring to when Kean had first come to meet them. Tabitha had looked totally shocked at Kean's reaction toward her bitchiness.

"And Stefan was very impressed that you picked out some great locations for his shoots," Ben said. "I saw a couple of his shots. Well done. You chose brilliantly, there." He nodded at Kean, clearly impressed.

"You *saw* them?" Kean looked horrified.

Ben pulled out his cell. "He was so excited about them that he wanted to show me. I can see why he was so enthusiastic, too. And he's not the only one." He swiped the screen a couple of times and passed his phone to Kean.

Isla looked over his shoulder as he gaped at the pictures on the screen. Her heartbeat was deafening. Although she was modeling the clothes, it was her expression that caught the eye. Even to her own mind, she looked beautiful. Her face was relaxed, her lips slightly apart and her eyes were so dreamy that they stole the picture. Her memory went back to the shoot. The first was in the evening in the woodland glade. The moon shone on her hair and shadows surrounded them, but her face seemed to glow. She'd been thinking about Kean at the time. She'd actually been looking at him when Stefan had taken the shots on the mountain. In one of them, she looked so melancholy and she remembered feeling that he didn't like her or want her there.

"They're beautiful," Kean murmured before passing the cell back.

"Miss Trotter thought so, too," Aidan piped up. "She rang to say how enthralled she was with them and asked if it would be possible to use our land again in the future. I wondered if we might come to some arrangement to use it to promote the ranch, too."

Heat seared through her whole body as she flushed. Those pictures looked quite intimate, more like the cover of a romantic novel than a clothing shoot. Her chest ached from the weight of her heartbeat and she busied herself straightening up her cup and plate on the side table to avoid catching anyone's eye.

"Your wedding photos will be gorgeous," Josie chirped.

"Thank you," Isla whispered, not daring to look up. *Oh God, they've all seen the pictures. I wonder what they all thought of them?*

Josie started collecting up the dishes "I'll make more coffee."

Kean prefers tea. He was obviously too polite to mention it. Her mind drifted back to the first time she had made him a cup of coffee, automatically assuming that's what he preferred. She had been standing in his doorway waiting for him to come back from tending the horses. He had looked so handsome tramping through the snow, and when he'd seen her, his whole face had lit up.

The fire in her stomach reignited and she glanced over at him, surprised to see that he was already gazing at her with that same expression. She squeezed his hand, wishing she could give him a loving, lingering kiss on his—

"Not for me. Thanks, Josie. I'd better get back to work," Jarrod announced, standing.

Isla balked, suddenly remembering where they were.

"Yes, of course." Kean quickly placed his plate on the tray.

"Not you," Cordell assured him, with a smile. "We thought you'd want to take the rest of day off to celebrate."

Kean looked really proud when he turned to face Isla, who beamed back at him.

"That's very kind of you, boss. I appreciate it. We both do." Kean actually blushed as he spoke.

Cordell stood. "Oh, that's not exactly what I meant about celebrating," he said, looking over at Isla. "Although the fact that you've decided to get married and settle down around here totally emphasizes my wisdom in making this decision." He looked quite proud of himself.

Kean's whole body tensed as he slowly stood, facing his boss.

Cordell nodded. "Yup, I've decided to give you the assistant foreman's job—if you still want it, of course?"

Kean's mouth gaped open for a moment and the room fell silent. "Yes," he managed, at last. "Yes, of course I want it. Yes, please." He nodded as Cordell came over and shook his hand, patting him on the back.

"Apart from everything else, we were real impressed that you volunteered for the job of taking care of our visitors, and you did great, by all accounts."

"He certainly did," Isla agreed, standing up to give Kean a big hug.

"Thank you," Kean replied, still looking totally stunned at his boss.

Everyone was on their feet again, shaking Kean's hand and hugging Isla once more.

"We do this at every given opportunity," Jarrod explained. He was a good-looking guy with an impish grin. "Any excuse'll do."

"He's right," Josie agreed, giving Isla another hug.

"Well, I think I can handle that," she said, hugging her back. It felt wonderful to get so close to people, and these folk sure seemed friendly.

"So, what are your plans?" Maggie asked, excitedly. "I presume you'll be going back to Sioux Falls to tie everything up? Then, of course, you've got to get all your stuff into Kean's place—and what about the wedding?"

"Ooh, yes." Josie joined in, her eyes shining. "The wedding. Well, I guess you've got your photographer organized. What about the rest?"

Kean's eyes darted to her. He looked apprehensive and she knew he would be worried about the money. They simply couldn't afford to get married right away, and that was fine by her. If, on the other hand, they suddenly found that they were in a hurry to marry then they would cross that bridge when they came to it. They would both be earning, and with his promotion, things should be a little easier.

"One thing at a time," she replied, putting up her hand to placate them. "Of course, I do have to do all that, as well as start my new job, but our first priority is a trip to North Dakota."

Kean stared at her and she turned to face him.

"Really?" he whispered.

She nodded. "We have to see your dad," she said softly, taking his hand. "I just know he'll be so proud of you."

Two for Trinity

Excerpt

Chapter One

"Hey-oll—you didn't tell us she was *that* cute!" Jarrod whistled as the petite, pink-haired girl climbed down from the train.

"Behave," Frank murmured under his breath as they walked toward her. "Remember what I told you."

Cordell rolled his eyes at his buddy, shaking his head in disbelief, but said nothing. Trust Jarrod… He gazed over at the girl and had to admit she was beautiful.

"Trinity, my, how you've grown." Sylvia was the first to approach the elfin girl, and the hug she gave her niece looked like it might snap her right in two.

"Aunt Sylvia, it's so nice to see you again." Trinity smiled, although her eyes maintained a melancholy expression. "And Uncle Frank, how good of you to fetch me. I was expecting to call a cab. How's your arm?" She frowned as she studied his left arm, encased in a sling across his chest.

Frank stood forward and gave her a hug, too. "It's fine, sugar. Don't you worry about that. I just fell a little awkwardly, the doctor said. Dang horse got spooked by a mouse or something and reared up suddenly. I didn't realize what was happening until I hit the ground." He chuckled. "Still, like I always say, where there's no sense, there's no feeling." He tipped his head as he let her go. "This here's Jarrod and Cordell." He gestured toward the two guys who stepped forward to join them.

Cordell watched Jarrod smile broadly at the pretty waif and cringed inside, unsure of how she would react to them. To his surprise, she held out her hand.

"Pleased to meet you. I'm Trinity Ellis," she said.

Jarrod seemed a little bemused as he shook her hand, though he was still smiling. "Jarrod Parker. Good to meet you, darlin'."

Cordell noticed her blush slightly before she turned to him, holding that hand out again.

"Hi Trinity, I'm Cordell Bray." He took her tiny hand in his, surprised that such a little woman had such a firm shake. She wore bright pink nail varnish that matched her hair, and her palm was warm and soft against his skin. He couldn't resist prolonging their shake a little as he continued, "Welcome to Cavern County."

She gave him a shy smile before withdrawing it. "Thank you."

"We came to carry your bags—and to do the driving, of course," Jarrod told her, glancing around.

"Oh, that's very kind. But I've only got this." She had a yellow, oversized handbag she was clinging to for dear life. "Everything else is gone." Tears filled her big, green eyes as she said it, and Cordell's heart went out to her.

"Well, let's get you home and settled in," Sylvia offered quickly, throwing an arm around Trinity and leading her toward the car. "I'll bet you haven't eaten in a while, have you?"

Cordell hung back a little as Frank followed the women.

"Looks like she hasn't eaten in a month of Sundays," Jarrod whispered, getting closer to his friend.

"Shh." Cordell rolled his eyes again. Jarrod was a lovely guy, but tact had never been his strong point.

"I'm only saying," Jarrod said, holding his hands up in surrender. "She seems like she'll get blown away if the wind springs up."

"Cut it out," Cordell murmured. "You know dang well she's been through hell and back. The last thing she needs is your smart-ass comments. And don't think I didn't notice you giving her the eye, either. She's off limits, remember?"

"She's still beautiful. You can't deny that," Jarrod muttered with his sing-song tone. "I saw the way you gawked at her, bro. You can't tell me you don't fancy her."

"That's not the point. Just cut it out, will you?" Cordell was muttering through clenched teeth as they neared the car.

Jarrod grinned.

Cordell sighed.

"Stop worrying," Jarrod whispered into his ear before disappearing around the other side of the car.

Cordell couldn't help smiling as he climbed into the driver's seat. Nothing fazed Jarrod. That was one of the many things he liked about his best friend.

"I've got the guest room all ready for you," Sylvia was telling Trinity as they drove toward Pelican's Heath.

"That's very nice of you," Trinity replied, in a small voice. She was sitting in between her uncle and aunt, who seemed to dwarf her, although they weren't exactly large people.

Cordell watched her through his rear-view mirror. She looked bewildered and he realized she must still be in shock after what had happened. "Do you like to ride, Trinity?" he asked, trying to keep the conversation light.

"Yes, I used to," she told the back of his head. "I haven't ridden for quite a while, though. Think I might be a bit rusty by now." Her voice sounded a little more cheerful, and he noticed in the rear-view mirror how she flushed slightly.

"Well, you'll get plenty of opportunity in Pelican's Heath," Jarrod offered. "Although I'd advise you to stay on the horse. Your uncle's method of riding isn't quite what we'd recommend."

They all laughed, and even Trinity sniggered, Cordell noticed. *Good.*

"I'll have you know that wasn't my fault, young man," Frank admonished, playfully.

Jarrod turned to face him. "What? Surely, you're not blaming that poor horse, Frank?"

Cordell glanced over to see the fake expression of shock on Jarrod's face as his buddy put his hands on his cheeks.

Trinity giggled. It was quiet, but it was definitely a giggle.

"That's not what I said and you know it," Frank protested with a tut. He was clearly well-used to Jarrod's teasing.

"Sounded that way to me. What do you think, Trinity?" Jarrod goaded.

"I'm not getting involved," she told him. "I wasn't there, remember?"

"None of us were," Cordell offered, still watching her in the mirror. "In fact, we've got our suspicions that there wasn't even a horse involved at all. Seems to us your Uncle Frank might have had a little too much of his elderflower wine and simply fell over his own feet or something."

Jarrod hooted with laughter, and Cordell was pleased to see Trinity snigger, too. Her face seemed a little more relaxed now, and she was even more beautiful.

"That's a load of baloney and you know it," Frank protested, shaking his head. He was in his seventies, very well-dressed and had an authoritative air about him. Luckily, he also had a keen sense of humor.

"Oh, Frank, you know the guys are only kidding," Sylvia soothed him with a smile. She turned to Trinity. "They do this all the time, hon. You'll soon get used to it."

Trinity smiled, and Cordell noticed her glance up at him in the mirror then blush as she quickly turned away, obviously seeing that he was watching her. He grinned. She was a hard one to figure out. Her bright pink hair and nails gave the impression of a girl who oozed confidence, although she seemed anything but right now. He hoped that spending some time in Cavern County would help her recover from her ordeal and get back to her normal self — whatever that might be.

"Here we are," Frank announced as they pulled up on the drive outside his large house. "Let's get you inside, young lady. You must be worn out."

"No, I'm fine, honestly, Uncle Frank. I slept on the train," Trinity said.

Jarrod was already waiting to help Sylvia and Trinity out of the car so Cordell slowly made his way toward the house where Frank was unlocking the front door.

"I don't like it," the older man whispered. "I know she's just lost her home, but I reckon there's more to it than that. She used to be so bubbly and lively. Hell, it was hard to get a word in edgeways last time she was here. I'm gonna get to the bottom of all this if it kills me." His face tightened as he spoke.

Cordell frowned, but, noticing the women catching up to them, said nothing.

"I'll put the coffee on," Frank offered as they all piled into the hallway. It was a beautiful home, with high ceilings and large rooms.

"Let me show you your room," Sylvia told Trinity with a smile. She led her up the stairs while the guys went through to the kitchen.

"Where have you been hiding her?" Jarrod asked, hoisting himself up to sit on the counter. His long legs dangled and he rolled up the sleeves of his white cotton shirt to reveal his ripped arms.

"I told you. She lives in Nebraska," Frank told him gruffly. "She used to come out here for holidays and stuff when she was growing up, but since she's started working, we've hardly seen her."

"She's sure grown into a gorgeous woman," Jarrod remarked.

Cordell was expecting Frank to berate Jarrod, but instead, the old man frowned thoughtfully. "She has." He nodded.

"But she's got a boyfriend, right? I noticed she's wearing a ring with a heart on it."

Cordell stared pointedly at Jarrod, recalling how Frank had filled them in on the situation earlier. "Here, let me help." He took out the coffee cups and pointed to a high stool where Frank obediently plunked himself down with a sigh.

"That ring was her momma's. It's probably the only thing she's got left of her now." He pursed his lips. "She did have a boyfriend, though. I presume they're still together."

"Then where the hell is he?" Jarrod fumed. "He should be with her right now, not leaving her to deal with all this by herself. What sort of man is he?"

Frank shook his head. "I never met him."

"Maybe that's part of the problem," Cordell offered. "If it was a bad split, it could have left her in a state, without her home going up in flames on top of it all. I think we need to tread carefully for a while, at least until we know the situation." He gave Jarrod one of his *I hope you're listening to this* stares before resuming preparation of the drinks.

He could feel Jarrod staring at the back of his head and knew his buddy had gotten his message loud and clear, although Cordell realized Jarrod wouldn't like it. Despite being one of the biggest flirts in Cavern County, Jarrod had a heart of gold. Cordell could see he liked Trinity—who wouldn't?—but he would need to tread carefully to avoid upsetting her. Jarrod's stunning appearance never failed to turn women weak at the knees, but in Trinity's case, that was the last thing she needed. The poor girl looked weak enough already.

He'd noted that Jarrod listened intently when Frank had told them last night that he would need a helping hand today, and he guessed the old man wasn't just referring to physical help. The poor guy had turned pale when he had explained to them that his niece had recently lost her home when a gas pipe exploded right outside her apartment building. Sylvia's sister — Trinity's mom — had passed away a few years ago, and the girl's dad hadn't been on the scene for a long while before that. Frank and Sylvia were worried sick about their niece and had insisted that she come to stay with them for a while. They were determined to care for her whether she wanted them to or not. She was quite independent, apparently, so had been a little reluctant to take them up on their offer.

It was hard to imagine Trinity as being a self-reliant chatterbox. Her face was pale and tired and her tiny frame made her seem fragile and weak. She was wearing jeans and a white T-shirt with Converse sneakers, and if it weren't for her bright pink hair, she would simply blend into any crowd. Her penchant for vivid pink made him think there was much more to Trinity Ellis than her manner suggested...

While the coffee pot gurgled away, Cordell turned around to face Frank, who looked lost in his thoughts as he sat at the counter staring into space. "How long will she be staying here?" he asked.

Frank quickly started in surprise, as though dragging himself from his muse. "As long as we can get her to," he murmured, half to himself, Cordell surmised.

"You said she worked from home. Has she got anything to go back to Nebraska for?" Jarrod frowned.

"I don't know. I suppose it hinges on this guy of hers," Frank replied. "If it's serious, she might want to get back to him as soon as she can." He pursed his lips thoughtfully. "It depends how she feels."

Cordell felt a jolt in his stomach at the thought of her boyfriend abandoning her at a time like this. "Can't be much of a man if he doesn't stick around when she needs him," he muttered.

"Ain't that the truth?" Jarrod chimed in with a sneer.

"Now, come on, guys. We don't know the whole story. Let's not jump to conclusions, shall we? There could be a perfectly good explanation as to why he's not here." Frank put a hand up to pacify them as he stood.

"I can't think of anything that would be counted as a good reason for not being with a girl when she needs him," Jarrod protested. "Any guy worth his salt would rush to be with her at a time like this. That girl needs comforting, looking after. Whoever this guy is, I could punch his dang lights out for not being there for her. He doesn't deserve a girl like Trinity. I don't care what his excuse is, it's not good enough. What sort of guy leaves a girl right after her home gets burned down?"

A sudden noise from the doorway made them all turn around.

"A dead one," Trinity replied.

More books from
Totally Bound Publishing

Book one in The Cowboys of Cavern County series

She can hide her secrets, but not her heart…

Book two in The Cowboys of Cavern County series

Looks can be deceptive – but a deceitful ex with a grudge can be downright dangerous.

Addie isn't shy about hooking up with rancher Bodie, even if he has a reputation as Mr. Unlucky. Can they change each other's fortunes?

All he needs is a second chance.

About the Author

Bella Settarra

Bella Settarra is a British Erotic Romance author and lives in the beautiful English countryside.

She has several published novels to date, with subject matter including cowboys, BDSM and Myth/Fantasy. She has also written short stories for anthologies and has even had some raunchy poems published.

She likes to keep busy, cramming as much into each day as she possibly can, while battling—and is determined to win—against breast cancer. She loves to hear from her readers, so please get in touch!

Bella Settarra loves to hear from readers. You can find contact information, website details and an author profile page at https://www.totallybound.com/

Home of Erotic Romance